hello

# Tales from the Casebook of
# D.I. SNAITH

As told to Dan Evans

For the Victims

Also By this author:
More Tales From the Casebook of
DI Snaith

# CONTENTS

# NOW. OR THEN. OR SOON.

I came upon his cabin in an instant. Two rabbits hung from its gutter, the mist dripping off their fur. On the stoop foam rubber spilled from a knackered armchair, beside it a rusty biscuit tin a quarter full of acorns.

Two years of query, bribe and hunch to find this clearing in the trees yet still I faltered, knuckles unable to swing that last inch to the door. At the moment I still had the myth. And what a myth it was. Did I really want to swap it for the man?

As though in answer to my question the rain began to fall in earnest. I took a breath, once more felt for the notebook in my pocket, then banged hard on the twisted boards. To the sound of heavy footsteps I scraped the forest from my boots.

*DI Snaith. Far from the best of men…*
*…but a damn good copper.*

# THE DEAD DON'T WED

*'He broke every rule in the book...*
*and then he broke the book'*

THE CAR. 5.42pm

Detective Inspector Snaith cleared the window with a rub of his cuff and stared out at the white stretched limousines that snaked off into the distance, his own just another segment in this seemingly endless tapeworm of masculine bonhomie.

So here they were. 'STAG'. Junction 8a of the M█. A place as tasteless as a petrol station pasty where lads in their last days of freedom fulfilled the wildest desires of their unfettered imaginations. Provided that those desires chiefly comprised of go-included carting, strippers, and drinking.

His focus switched and he caught his faint reflection in the glass. Blotchy and pudge-eyed from last night's session, even in the dim yellow of the courtesy light his tongue looked rough as a Boot Camp towel. That will do for now, he thought, exhaling so condensation spared him the sight. He snuck a glance at his two colleagues, slumped on the broad back seat of this daft car:

DI Wilton, not that tired cliché of a Maverick who gets results. Wilton was different; he was the Maverick who *didn't* get results. A man addicted to bizarre surgical twiddles he believed would boost his arrest rate, but never seemed to.

Next to Wilton was DI Harris, a gangly collection of minor ailments wrapped in a beige trench coat, pockets bulging with decongestants and nebulizers.

With a start the monstrous gas-guzzler pounced forward and DI Harris's plastic breasts tumbled to the floor, the hidden camera within clicking like a jogger's flip flop.

DI Wilton raised a metal paw and scratched his chest, the cheaply stenciled T Shirt losing a few more flakes of its hopeful mantra:

'Sex Instructor, First Lesson Free'

Snaith felt the sweat on his forehead and reached for the window. Before it was a quarter down the beggars were there, like pigeons round a biscuit. Barefoot, cataracted, thin as a 'Murder She Wrote' plotline. He upped the glass and the hands withdrew, along with their multiple wares: Inflatable sheep, underpants bearing the edict, 'Home of Rover the Great Pussy Hunter', and wigs, so many blue wigs.

The air in the limo was heavy with the stench of stale sweat and beer-burps, and with its fetid lingerings came memories of his ex wife Eunice. Snaith fought back a lump in his throat the size of a baked potato and remembered the days that preceded his own doomed union. His proposal in the bistro - he'd got down on one knee and looked her straight in the eye - having first climbed on the table first to accommodate the vertical discrepancy.

'Eunice', he'd uttered, deftly removing his right foot from her tiramisu, 'Would you do me the honour of making me the happiest man alive...'

'For the last time', spat Snaith's flame-haired nemesis, 'I'm not having any damn breast implants…'

'No no. Would you do me the honour of becoming… Mrs DI Snaith. Watson to my Holmes, Cagney to my Lacey…' The same-sex crime partner analogies were far from ideal, but he was flustered and 'Moonlighting' had failed to spring to mind.

THE ENTRANCE TO STAG 6.38pm
Finally they rolled through the gates, and beneath the constantly clicking sign –

'Welcome To STAG: Copulation 2,437…438…439…'

- surely the first of many hilarious jokes celebrating the rich bawdy heritage of Anglo-Saxon wedlock. Times had surely changed. Snaith recalled his own Stag night, a modest affair: a few pints with the lads topped off nicely by a round or two of 'Keith Moon' with the Desk Sergeant.[1]

The motorised folly that bore the three detectives lurched on past crowds of men in kilts, T Shirts proclaiming nicknames, and the ubiquitous blue wigs, perhaps a nod to more ancient Britons smeared with woad for battle. But who was he to criticize? Was it

---

[1] *A game played to pass the time in many Police stations. Officers enter an occupied cell, a truncheon in each hand, and attempt to reenact the errant Who Drummer's vigorous playing style.*

really any different to Hemmingway wrestling marlin from the depths on a boat tossed about by Poseidon's fickle whim, or Donald Campbell skimming the surface of Lake Coniston, cheeks flapping with the G force. They were all just guys, guys cutting loose.

Snaith took a last look behind him, just making out the entrance to 'HEN' (Junction 8b), its queue of bubble-gum pink gas-guzzlers crammed with bethonged high-heeled sirens. Plus a fair few foghorns.

Once inside, STAG and HEN, much in the style of a Venn diagram, melded into one. 2 square miles of migrant staff scuttling about service tunnels, dispensing cholesterol and liquid amnesia through slots cut in shatterproof Perspex, while neon signs tempted the temporary residents:

> *Brathausen, Ice Filtered for a cleaner taste'*
> *HufferBrau – for best results, mix with friends'*

And the arguably less subtle:

> *Lambruno girls do it in their vaginas'.*

The three detectives eyed the plastic teats that seemed to sprout at random from the walls: a brewery trick to extract all remaining shrapnel from the tippler's pocket. Thanks to the marvels of the digital age the thirsty reveler could feed in an amount however small; half a Credit, 7 cents, even a single coin, then kneel on the grubby plastic cushion beneath and suckle the corresponding quantity of beer dispensed from the building's synthetic nipples.

STAG was beyond the law, this the first incursion since its opening 2 years prior, despite many reports of drunken anarchy within. After all, it had brought peace to the high streets of England. Besides, the more nervous reveler could always pay 800 Credits for an Emergency Necklace (Cr700 returned if unused), rescue guaranteed with just one press of its big red button.

An earpiece crackled. 'It's the Gaffer', said Snaith, 'he wants us to instigate camouflage protocol'.
A pause, Snaith and Wilton both blurted, 'Bagsee-not-me' and Harris frowned; he'd dropped his guard a second too long. He dutifully lowered his trousers and squeezed his bare buttocks through the window, the other two authenticating the moon with a lackluster *'Waheeeey!'* Surely just the first drop in a monsoon of testosterone-fuelled folly set to blight their weekend.

SCUFFLES FUN PUB 9:04pm
'8 dead. In as many weeks', DI Harris mused, wiping drops of luminous blue alco-jelly from the case file with a hankie that was surely just days from retirement. 'These guys, there *must* be a link'.

'We should go', muttered Snaith, 'this is, well, it's a little distracting'.

17

On the nearby stage some Stags were playing 'Churchill'. To the cheers of the crowd, they'd invert themselves on a stool, naked from the waist down, an eye drawn on each buttock. Then came the classic victory hand gesture and a strain, followed by prizes for the best cigar effect. The three left to the sound of yet another dull thud in a bucket.

'It's just a guess but I think I've found a link' said Snaith. 'I suspect that all the victims… were arseholes'.

## SQUEALERS KARAOKE BAR 9:47pm

The 'Stage'. A stout post the circumference of the circle defined by a yodeler's hands rose five feet from the floor: the microphone. Strangely inconsistent in design - one of the few things in STAG to actually already resemble a penis stood there unadorned by what would have been easy to achieve phallic embellishments.

DI Harris had only popped in to use the gents but there didn't seem to be one, and now he hid beneath a table, trapped by a sudden ingress of drunks. It had been an uncomfortable half hour, the highlight a rendition of the Bangles' 'Eternal Flame' where the singer had lain on his back with a lighter held to his buttocks, and strained till his face was scarlet. The resulting fireball had a Hen upending a beer jug in a desperate attempt to extinguish her veil. Luckily she'd invested in an Emergency Necklace – and only moments after her frantic button-pressing had come the deafening *'Thwucker!'* of a chopper before two men in orange body suits had tazered their way through the crowd and dragged her off to safety. Twenty minutes later it was Gloria Gaynor being slain on the stage.

*'First I was afraid, I was petrified'*, bellowed two mid-twenties chums, *'kept thinking I could never live without you by -'*

Wallop! They were down, felled by territorials from the Toon Army. They clearly hadn't known the tradition - put on, 'I will survive' and a race was on to prove you wouldn't. It was similar folly to choose Queen's 'Don't Stop Me Now'.

*'Whooooareya? Whooooareya? Whoooooooareya?'* cheered the new arrivals into the chin-high polymer bollard, resplendent in their 70 Credit-a-piece black and white striped tops, thin as carrier bags, but surely costing 5 times as much to manufacture. DI Harris saw his moment, and shot out from his sanctuary with the speed of a gingered horse, stumbling off down the street through the yeasty sludge.


TITTERS COMEDY CLUB 10:16pm

DI Snaith hobbled to a table, his mind a bran tub. The solution was somewhere in his head, but try as he might he just couldn't get his hands in to rummage round and find it. The three had split to cover ground, and Snaith had spent the last hour trudging the litter-strewn streets gulping Manhattans from a Thermos.

His bleary eyes surveyed the room: Stags poured lager from breast shaped jugs, Hens poured white wine from bottles resembling male genitalia. He was detecting a theme.

On the stage, behind perforated Perspex stood the comic, eyes lifeless as finger prod-holes in a sponge cake. He quizzed the front row.

*'Where you from?'* / *'St Albans'* / *'What a shithole!'*

The audience howled. Snaith's head span. St Albans was nice enough, Roman ruins, an art-house cinema, a diverse selection of restaurants.

*'St Albans eh'* the comic pressed on. *'Ba da bow bow bow bow bow bow bow!'*

Snaith knew the tune instantly - the banjo riff from 'Deliverance': John Boorman's darkly disturbing 1972 wilderness classic in Panavision. The audience roared. Snaith was baffled. Surely there could be no comparison, *even* allowing for comedic exaggeration, between the deplorable brutality of backwoods Appalachia and a cosmopolitan commuter town with a 20-minute train connection to central London. It was almost as though the comic would have responded with the same riff *whatever* town had been mentioned.

The Detective's gaze came to rest on a woman. With a man, but on her own. Stroking his shoulder, his head lolling like Stevie Wonder circa 'I Just Called to Say I Love You'. There was something not quite right. Snaith's eyes narrowed, then to avoid suspicion he closed them fully to give any onlooker the impression he was merely blinking - a sweet trick he'd picked up at Hendon Police College.

The crowd roared once more and he turned back to the stage. The balloons were out. The comic toyed with a long thin one in particular. Snaith's detective senses tingled, straining to second-guess the outcome of this skilled inflatable sculpting.

'What am I doing?' barked the comic, holding the long balloon tangential to his body at groin level, as though, Snaith deduced, in imitation of a penis, before furiously rubbing it with his right hand. Snaith slammed his palms over his ears and dropped to his knees as the audience response pushed into white noise. He saw feet swing past. Stumbling piss-stained loafers led by discreet pink training shoes. Flat shoes. On a woman. A woman in HEN?!

Snaith leapt to his feet and spun to see the now-empty table of his lonely female muse. She was gone. And with her the man. Suddenly Snaith knew what was wrong. She was… Sober! He staggered from Titters and scanned the street outside like a hawk. Not a hawk in flight, but one sitting on a post about the height of a man. Yes. She was sober. But She was nowhere to be seen.

He'd never felt more an outsider. The comic's skillful display of self-stimulation through the medium of balloons hadn't helped. It seemed Snaith didn't even do that like other men: not much bothering with

21

the lower half, only really concentrating on the far end.

He shuffled through the gunk of chips and wigs that iced the street, dodging the 'Rollers' working through the night turning the inebriated onto their fronts that they might not choke on the Alcopops and deep-fried dross any self-respecting body would rightfully reject. Not so much compassion on STAG's part as a guard against litigation and bad press.

AN ALLEY, A BRIEF STUMBLE FROM TITTERS. 11:04pm

The downcast DI leant sweating against a wall, his piss beating out a bossanova beat on a pile of yellow cartons. As the trickle slowed he became aware he wasn't alone in the alley. Shooting a glance into the blackness his heart pounded in his chest, the beat alarming but the location reassuring. Two silhouettes seemed to dance slowly in the distance, their moves accompanied by muffled choking.

*'Whahaaaay!*

Snaith spun about and found himself facing a tottering lad in a gorilla suit, its chest hair matted with vomit.

'Shhhhhhh!'

*'Whahaaaay!'* insisted the lad, pointing at Snaith's crotch. The detective briskly cajoled his member back in and upped the zip.

'Shhhhh! You idiot'.

At that the lad's jocular manner inverted.

*'Oh I geddit. You... You-think-yaw-better-than-me. Dontcha? Dontcha?!'*

Snaith dodged a floppy jab, yanked the boy behind a bin, then peered round into the darkness. The choking had stopped and a shadowed head had turned toward them.

*'Wah -'*

He slapped his hand tight over the boy's mouth and pulled him back out of sight. After what seemed an age the gargled tussle down the alley resumed. Snaith peered round the bin to again observe this toxic embrace. The distant curvaceous outline looked up and a body fell from Her shadowed hands. Time seemed to stand still and Snaith fancied he felt a moment between them, as though they were somehow kindred spirits. Suddenly he realised the boy was now motionless between his fingers, limp as a homework excuse.

*'Shit!'*

He dropped the lifeless lad and gulped. Still, these things happen. Quite often. He knew a wave of guilt was coming, but also knew it wouldn't overwhelm him. DI Snaith had learnt to surf that wave, and maybe that was ultimately his tragedy.

He stuffed the body into the rancid sludge pooled beneath the huge wheeled bin and took to his heels, pausing only to improvise a cross from two lolly-sticks as a mark of respect.

The portly policeman leapt rivulets of dirty fluids with an ursine flourish till he stood astride a second corpse: that of the loll-headed man from Titters. A crunch of broken glass from the far end of the alley brought him back to the now and he was away once more, chasing the fleeing female form into the 'town' beyond.

The vein in Snaith's forehead throbbed as he ran, pounding hard like rain on a burger-van roof as he chased the receding shape through the grid of streets, their rigid order mocked by the alcohol fueled anarchy that raged about. Rounding a corner he ploughed straight into a heaving crowd. Once more She was gone.

After wiping the sweat from his eyes with a stumbling Stag's Batman cape the Detective took in his surroundings. It was one of the Go-Cart tracks... the crowd all shouting at someone cowering on a two-story flat roof. One lad clawed his way up a drainpipe toward the figure but as he neared the top it stood... the crowd roaring as it puffed up its throat to the size of a watermelon. It was DI Wilton. The lad fell backwards into his mates. A cheer, and then another began the ascent. It was only a matter of time.

Snaith ran to a nearby vending machine and rammed in a fist full of coins. It whirred and clunked, then coughed out 5 greasy balls of deep fried breadcrumbs each about the size of a Munchkin's fist. Pausing only to baulk at the smell he jammed them into two of a dozen polystyrene trays that tumbled from one of several filthy openings, then stuffed those into his pockets.

The burly cop quickly forced his way through the crowd to the base of the drainpipe and became the next to brave the climb. The grease on his hands hampered his progress but two feet from the top, to the screams all below, the familiar tail of DI Wilton appeared. Snaith took hold of it and was soon on the rooftop with his ailing comrade.

'I've been such a fool', gabbled Wilton.

'There isn't time', bellowed Snaith, turning to see hands feeling their way over the parapet. 'That grille up there... climb on my back and prise it off'.

Wilton obliged, and the slotted metal oblong clattered down beside them. Snaith grabbed it, then slapped it across the face now looming up over the roof's edge which then dropped out of sight. The crowd below roared. He had raised the stakes, there could be no going down now.

'That's our way out', hissed Snaith, throwing a look to the rectangular void the grille had once fronted. Wilton looked down at his ample midriff and buried his head in his paws. Snaith yanked the greasy snacks from his pocket and threw some at Wilton.

'Rub them... rub them on your widest parts'.

DUCT 7, BRANCH 21. 11:23pm

Progress was slow. Wilton squeaked his way in front, forming an airtight seal, as did Snaith behind, leaving him with just the 3 feet of duct between them from which to take his air. An air befouled by frequent nervous contributions from beneath his colleague's twitching tail.

DUCT 7, MAIN. 11:44pm
The two detectives dropped a foot in the darkness into a larger duct running at right angles to the first, now able to crawl on their knees.

'Ventilation', wheezed Snaith. 'For the Service Areas. It has to be'.

'There was this girl... in one of the Go Carts. With an L Plate on her front', mumbled Wilton.

'A Hen'.

'I wasn't thinking straight. I just thought, Learner driver... unaccompanied by a full license holder and, and... call it instinct... I cautioned her. As soon as they knew I was a Rozzer it all kicked off... I got to a car but on the first straight my tail, my *damn* stupid tail got wrapped round the axle. By the time I'd yanked it free I had no option but to climb'.

Snaith bit his lip. He'd never seen the benefit to policing of adding 3 feet of ginger fur but Wilton had been adamant it needed doing. Hell, the damn thing wasn't even prehensile.

As they shimmied along the duct the temperature rose, Snaith wedging an empty polystyrene tray beneath each knee to hold back the heat. The two men heaved through their sweat, a background hiss of white noise rising in volume. A thin yellow light thickened slices of steam that filled the duct ahead. Arriving at a large louvered vent their laboured breathing momentarily halted as they gazed in awe through the metal slats. The source of the heat and noise lay bare in front of their disbelieving eyes.

Below them a vat the size of an Olympic swimming pool bubbled furiously, filled to a foot from its brim with what could only be cooking oil. Immense conveyor belts coughed shapeless lumps into its depths, flinging up broken ropes of scalding yellow hell as they plipped through it's fevered surface. Snaith prodded Wilton and gestured to the far end of the pool. Through the mist, in the calmer depths away from the conveyors they could make out what seemed to be boats. Stout little craft, 10, maybe 12 of them, their pilots men... women... who could say? Clad from head to foot in a thick shapeless fabric, eyes invisible behind steamed up helmets. Two per boat, one at the rear propelling with a sculling action, the other at the sharp end scooping crisp brown shapes from the liquid beneath with something resembling a metal lacrosse stick.

They had truly found the Devil's caterers. Like some hideous travesty of Willy Wonka's factory, though Snaith was keen to note not quite similar enough to cause copyright problems were his escapades to be later dramatized in visual media. DI Wilton let out a whimper, and spat on his paws to cool them. The pair shuffled on, the heat receding, the noise replaced by another higher pitched hiss.

30 metres on they passed the next vent, once more stunned by the view. Yet more conveyors, set between rows of nozzles relentlessly spraying what seemed to be batter, the belts heavy with assorted rubbish… lumps of plasterboard, old shoes, a tatty handbag. Snaith fingered one of the broken fried balls in his pocket. Breaking apart the coating he felt laces.[2]

Some time later, courtesy of the ventilation system, the two spent coppers had seen it all. Hectares of service areas interlocked with STAG and HEN, with no connection except Perspex windows in the bars, and the occasional reinforced door: discreet exits for the few who must ply their wares in the streets themselves - prostitutes, some adjusted, most in original condition, both donning luminous red conical hats. Pickpockets, Snaith assumed, having witnessed demonstrations through one of the grilles, presumably tolerated in exchange for some kind of commission.

---

[2] *(On his return Snaith alerted the relevant authority to the fried litter scandal. No further action - there was considered no case to answer. The frying process sterilized the contents so there was no threat to public safety. The vending machines never claimed they offered 'Food', only 'Fewd', 'Snackz' or 'Tucker'. It was also felt that highlighting the practice was poor reward for STAG and HEN's admirable advances in reaching ever-increasing recycling targets).*

And the Rollers, supplementing their tiny wage with stealings from the unconscious - watches, glasses, belly button fluff.

Now they stared through a hole, its vent already removed, into the dormant brain of the beast. 3 dozen phones and monitors. Bold text across one wall read -

## BOOKING OFFICE

Snaith waved his tiny torch about the floor of the vent and its kitten-weak light picked out footprints. Small, a training shoe. Size 4 maybe 5. It seemed they weren't the first to shuffle through these ducts.

JUNCTION OF DUCTS 7, 6 & 5. 12:32am

The pair lay wheezing in a shallow chamber, the metal beneath them now cool. Then suddenly came a faint nonsensical cry -

*'Whooooaaaargh!'*

'Which way?' whispered Wilton, with a voice now tired as a Fools-and-Horses Christmas Special.

'Shhhh', hissed Snaith. The distant moronic holler came once more. 'Here! It came from down here'.

★

A further 40 minutes crawling, knees aching like teenage heartbreak, and the weary Fuzz kicked out another vent. After deep gulps of the cool night air they flumped groundward onto a heap as soft as fresh bread. The sting of ammonia rose about them, and

Snaith remembered an illuminated sign from earlier that night –

> *'Dude Diapers: When you gotta go...*
> *...but you wanna stay'*

His earpiece crackled. Then wheezed and coughed. It was DI Harris.

## THE ALLEY A BRIEF STUMBLE FROM TITTERS. 12:48am

'Poor bastard', choked Harris, staring beneath the roller bin at the corpse in its filthy gorilla outfit.

'Erm... that's actually, well, call him 'Collateral Damage'', Snaith uttered apologetically with the sort of voice you'd use after letting one go in a busy lift. 'The other one, the *bad* one, that's further down'. Snaith met DI Harris's frown, held it a moment, then batted it off with an attempt at a carefree shrug.

## THE ALLEY. FURTHER DOWN. 12:50am

Wilton frisked the body of the loll-headed man from Titters Comedy Club, his stainless steel paws moving about it with the speed and tenderness of an Argentinean gigolo.

'Wallet's still here'.

'I disturbed them', said Snaith studying the Smurf blue face, its eyes bulging like a constipated Chihuahua.

'I think we have our murder weapon'. Wilton held aloft a paw, over it was draped a thong.

A revolver clicked, the three spun round on their haunches. There She was. Flat shoes, sober. Even in the near darkness Snaith could tell that She had all the right bits, and that most of them were in all the right places.

'Very clever', She hissed.

The three men crouched, trapped in her mesmerising gaze. As though rabbits, her eyes the headlamps of a car on a country road. A firm-thighed car with hair that tumbled down it's back. Police rabbits. Frozen.

'What to do, what to do', She mused, stepping back so Wilton's mirror-finish steel paw no longer compromised her dignity from its position on the ground beneath her skirt.

'But...' DI Harris broke the silence, 'why did you come back?'

'She needed ID', said Snaith, 'How else would *they* know She'd done her job?'

'Go on', she murmured.

Something about her hourglass figure told Snaith time was running out. He got slowly to his feet.

'It's a pretty sweet operation. We were right about the link lads'.

Harris and Wilton swapped puzzled glances.

'The victims *were* all arseholes. But not just arseholes in here, arseholes out there too, in the big wide world. So what She...'

'Think of all the fathers who see their daughter hitch up with a total arsehole... who have to welcome him to the family through gritted teeth. They'd do anything to....'

'Alright love, no need for the monologue, I have worked it out you know', snapped Snaith. 'She's an assassin. Frustrated soon-to-be fathers-in-law pay her to do away with morons before they can marry their daughters'.

A wry smile crept across the face of the teetotal temptress.

'Wilton, you saw how extensive those ducts were', Snaith still felt there were gaps to fill, 'it'd be a synch to infiltrate the booking system. Names, addresses, numbers... engineer a chance encounter with the old guys, probably in some pub drowning their sorrows at the prospect of bankrolling the imminent union... drop the idea in as a joke...'

She stepped forward.

*'He's just not good enough for my Janey, my Janey could do so much better',* She whimpered in a parody of tipsy bourgeois paternal angst. Suddenly she raised the gun 'Then again, I don't always need to be paid to kill'...

DIs Harris and Wilton backed away leaving Snaith firmly in her sights. She pulled back the little metal bit above the handle, and the three DIs cowered, no longer rabbits but mice. Snaith took a step back, treading on the corpse of Her previous prey, the loud *'Clack!'* emanating from his chest prompting DI Harris to once more fill his luckless hankie.

'You know I saw what you did with those big hands of yours', She whispered at DI Snaith, in a voice as husky as coconut casing. 'Why not come in with me, we could clean up in a place like this'.

Snaith thought about his meager police pension, an old age of Super Noodles and stalking Eunice. Would it be so bad? It could be argued it was a kind of public service. After all, these boys would be no real loss…

*Thwuckker! Thwuckker! thwuckkkker!*

…before they knew it the helicopter was overhead, and a steel cable ladder thrashed the air above their heads.

*'Son, show me your necklace…'*

A megaphone had never sounded so sweet.

In the full glare from above she raised the revolver to Snaith's temple… for a moment he felt sure he could see down its barrel… see the tip of the bullet that surely bore his name.

### THWUCKKER!

The chopper's downdraft tumbled litter all about, and suddenly a blue wig whipped up and wrapped itself about Her head like a vengeful squid. Snaith snatched the gun as She clawed at the strands of dirty blue nylon. Wilton fumbled about Her victim's chest then held up something that glinted in the dancing chopper-light – an Emergency Necklace! Thank God the boy had not just been an arsehole, but also a wuss.

Fifty pairs of red dots emerged from the darkness. Battery powered Devil horns; it could only mean one thing. The Hens had come! Harris had almost climbed the writhing ladder, Wilton was 8 rungs up. Snaith had his arm hooked over the lowest, dangling, his feet at head height, the rotors of the straining chopper barely drowning out the screeching of approaching Brides-to-be.

*'You can't just leave her there'* bellowed Wilton through the beaten air, *'Who knows what they'll do to her'.*

'We'll pick up the bits in the morning', rasped Snaith. He thought Wilton hadn't heard, but then came the reply –

*'You bastard, you're not just a pig... you're an animal!'*

Maybe he was right. She was now atop the huge bin, the Hens scratching at her legs, seemingly mystified by the lack of purple blotches.

Then their eyes met. Snaith dropped his hand and She took it. He grabbed his police badge from his inside pocket with his teeth and held it up to the glare above, a moment later spitting it out and roaring –

*'LETS GO!'*

The helicopter tottered upward into the night sky, finally free of the baying tarts beneath. Snaith took a last look at the mayhem below - the girls now yanking down the trousers of the two corpses in the alley. His eyes caught Hers again. And Hers his. Snaith's mind raced as Her lustrous brown locks danced in the wind. She smiled. Could this... could she... be his new Eunice? Snaith smiled back. A real smile, one that spoke of lazy bed-bound Sunday mornings, croissant flakes on the duvet, whiskey macs shared in the snug of a country pub. He had very expressive lips.

Then he felt the filthy grease still about his hands. And he felt Her fingers clutch ever tighter, hungry for traction. She stared at their slowly slipping union.

'You ate from the machines, didn't you?'

Snaith couldn't reply, focusing all his mind on tightening his grasp. But still, slow as a barge, she moved away.

'I always knew fried food would be the death of me' She uttered, then was gone, flicking fast toward the ground like a sneeze.

As the swaying ladder cleared the gates of STAG Snaith cried, cried like a baby chopping onions. The first time he'd done so in a year without the use of pepper spray.

## CASE CLOSED

# VIXEN OF DOCK GREEN

*'Lady Luck's had a facelift...*
*but she won't pay the bill'*

SOMEWHERE IN THE NORTH ATLANTIC.
2:05 pm.

Detective Inspector Snaith's eyes shot open as the frigid sea slapped his face. Choking on the salt he spun about and grabbed the man hoiking at his trouser waistband. Both he and his assailant tumbled back into the boat.

*'Damn you. Damn you to hell!'* yelled the figure in the ripped Kagoul now kneeling on the wet boards at Snaith's feet. *'I'm nearly there and YOU drop in. Well, if you think you're going to spoil things you've got another thing coming'.*

Snaith felt knuckles in his stomach, then he was on his back, pinned down while a fierce sun played peekaboo behind his tormentor's silhouette. Both gulped breaths in the gull-broken silence as the yellow disc ducked behind a cloud, giving Snaith a chance to study the face that loomed over him: Tired wired eyes, tatty beard, skin burnt and cracking, a passionate sun may well have kissed it but had clearly then moved straight on to 3rd Base.

A tear dripped onto the detective's chest then the man loosed his grip and leant back on his haunches.

'You *have* to go, else it won't count...it wont count', he mumbled, burying his face in his hands. '3 years preparation. I said I'd do it solo, I *have* to do it solo". The spent sailor took unsteadily to his feet, hobbled into the cabin then reappeared a moment later, grappling with the flyblown carcass of a 3-foot turtle.

Snaith lay still on the deck, having lost round 2 of his fight with sleep... and the events of the past few days danced once more through his dreams.

## THE CREMATORIUM, THREE DAYS PRIOR.

DI Snaith hung motionless, observing the tragic tableaux through mirrored glasses. Much-loved glasses, originals from his favourite show, 'Chips'. 3,868 Credits of drunken eBay purchase. He'd told ex-wife Eunice he'd pay anything for a pair, then, lo and behold, two days later they'd appeared for sale. He wasn't to know she'd been the one furiously bidding against him, that they were actually Cr3.99 from the covered market, or that it was her who had placed the ad. Nor did he know his bid had paid for the contract she'd put out on him, and hence the bullets still lodged in his colon that meant he could now only pass solids while partially inverted. Well, all marriages went through the odd rough patch.

The strange scene before him was based on a traditional funeral but was also so so different. It was all down to new emissions targets - these days if you wanted an actual cremation you not only had to keep the ashes, but the smoke as well. Occasionally you would still see a weeping spouse, a fist-full of strings leading 60 bobbing black balloons. Like some grotesque hawker at a fairground. A fairground... of Death!

Land prices had made burials a rarity, though cheap

plots might occasionally be found, the less squeamish sometimes prepared to sell space below flower beds or sitting rooms to help keep the bills at bay. There were even a few more ad hoc options - many a grieving relative had disembarked from a ferry minus the large trunk they'd boarded with - but on the whole it was either this, or fly tipping.

It was both simple and effective. Westerly winds would be forecast, and the despatches would start. The bereaved would gather around the giant black inverted funnel while beneath it dangled the deceased. A rope linked them to a helium balloon above the building, just large enough to carry their weight. Friends and family might throw a few rose petals, then the vicar would do his thing before releasing the corpse. Nearly departed became dearly departed, rising slowly up the spout and into the clouds, the breeze carrying them across the country, then over the Atlantic, until the release valve activated and they descended gracefully into the water.

Snaith squinted through the tint of his lens. The hymnbooks snapped shut; the late Mrs. Henderson clanked her way up the pipe, her nearest and dearest shuffling out to the patio to watch her head west, the undertaker delaying them a moment with small talk to ensure there'd be no accidental last upward glimpse of her knickers. He imagined her body drifting gently toward the steely grey Atlantic, the toes of the burial shoes skimming the surface, throwing up tiny wakes for a yard or two before she was smacked by a wave or melted into a swell. He pictured the sharks licking their lips. Did sharks have lips? Try as he might he just couldn't picture them kissing.

*Kchwhiiiiiiiiiiiiiiiiiiiiiiiiir Mhchenirrrrgggggg!*

And so it became the Detective's turn, the conveyor dragging him by the hanger in the back of his coat toward the upturned funnel. He must be still, no one must suspect.

His breathing was so slight as to be undetectable, the many hours training with wind chimes dangling from his nasal hair had clearly paid off. The trick is to overcome what is clearly a paradox and fill your mind with nothingness. A talent well-taught at Hendon Police College. And so the detective hung, still as four-day-old Cola. He had been the obvious choice. He could pass for dead most days. Hell, if you've nothing to live for, you're already halfway there. Besides, he knew well what a corpse felt like, having shared a bed with Eunice.

Balloon 'burials'. A far from perfect system. Charts. Air currents. Isobars. Science to mask the denial. Gull-pecked remains plagued the Azores. At first they were thought to be migrants drowning in attempts to reach Europe, so nothing was done. In part that was the purpose of the rings. Unspoken though it was everyone knew the gold band was to compensate any traumatised recipient following an unexpected change in wind direction. But therein lay the problem - if you had the stomach for it why not pop a balloon over Cornwall and prize the jewelry from a crumpled corpse?

But this was no robbery case. It was Murder. Snaith wasn't the first to perform in this pantomime; he was following in the footsteps of a young Detective Sergeant who'd played dead in the hope of stemming the petty thievery. He had gone missing. No body had been found; a baker in Polperro had been caught wearing his shoes but claimed they'd been found on the moor. The talk was of a tip off, his cover blown, his fresh-dead organs harvested and sold on the open market. Even a rumour of a kidney sold on Redruth market. Well it was Cornwall, anything was possible.

The young sergeant's probable death had hit Snaith hard. In the lad's 14 months at the Met they had become firm friends. Snaith and Eunice, in the glory days of their marriage (April-June the previous year) had taken him under their wing, Eunice trying to find the shy young man a girl. Taking him out night after night to restaurants, museums, cinemas, just on the off-chance he'd find a mate. And when the wrestling match they'd called a marriage fell apart the lad had been there for Snaith, spending hours alone with Eunice in ultimately doomed attempts to persuade her to part with his share of their stuff. He'd even broken the news to Snaith when Eunice had become pregnant by a mystery lover. And now, quite likely, his heart pumped in another man.

The vicar pressed a switch and Snaith's requested music faded in. The rousing theme from Radio 2's Sports Report. As the man of God busied himself moving floral truncheons Snaith snuck a glance about him. The Squad walked slowly in, this had to pass for the real thing, there had to be mourners.

DI Wilton, the maverick, chewing on a biro, his twelfth of the day. Building up a reservoir of ink to discharge as a cloaking device to disorientate suspects. The others just praying to God he wouldn't sneeze. Or fart.

The Gaffer, a man so wrinkled he could front a campaign for the Walnut Marketing Board. Fingertips yellow as yolk. His tumbling tears were real, 3 hours into his latest attempt to quit smoking and that monkey... that gorilla was on his back. If he'd had a time machine, he'd have gone back there and then to Plymouth Docks and beaten Walter Raleigh to a pulp on the gangplank. It would have robbed England of her chips but for him that was a price worth paying. Rocking back-and-forth in his brown 3-piece, beneath it a cat-suit stitched purely from Nicorette patches.

DI Harris stood behind the others, in a charcoal pin-striped, the hessian bag covering his head giving him the air of a Mafia scarecrow. Poor Harris, he'd crossed the mob one too many times (which is once) and now they were after him. He'd had no choice but to have his face surgically pixilated. The only way to see the old Harris now was through the frosted glass of a toilet window.

It may have been Snaith's funeral, but it was a toss up to say which of them was the most dead.

The cluster of weary lawmen jumped as the main door burst open and a black-caped figure entered, crossing the marble floor with the speed and deportment of a bin liner in a force eight, heels clacking like a football rattle. On reaching the funnel the spectre flung itself to the floor at DI Snaith's feet.

It was Eunice.

Snaith's heart leapt to two beats a minute - She'd always said they'd only get back together over his dead body. The policeman's wife, Vixen of Dock Green. Now clearly six month's gone with another man's child.

*'Nooooooooooooooooo!'* shrieked the husky strumpet, clawing the marble floor, rolling her teeth and gnashing her eyes, a volcano of emotion erupting wet mascara. The black widow grabbed Snaith's trousers as if her very life depended on it. Just as the mission's cover looked sure to be blown the Gaffer leapt like an asthmatic panther and a moment later she lay immobile, hands tied tight behind her back with DI Wilton's Tail.

Rising up the pipe Snaith strained to comprehend the turn of events. His ex back. But why? Maybe she still cared. Perhaps when all this was over they could make another go of things. Buy a farm. One in the country. He could get some pigs; she could knit stuff, his head in her lap, dodging the needles above... He'd happily raise the other man's child as his own. That would be fine: all the time in the world to destroy it's self-esteem. Could it work? Taylor to his Burton, Delilah to his Samson, Eunice to his Snaith.

As Snaith drifted over the memorial gardens he stared down at her. Krakatoa now just smoking. Lambert and Butler. And so the Detective wafted west, the motorway below... London a goldfish heading east, the fat ribbon of tarmac its dangling plop that trailed behind.

SOME TIME LATER

Detective Inspector Snaith was on his own now; the shoe with the tracking device to provide the failsafe link to The Squad having slipped off during his ex wife's frenzied display of all-consuming grief.

He needed a drink. The drifting DI pulled open his jacket to reveal a bullet-belt embossed with the words 'Welcome to Tijuana'. Snaith perused the miniatures it contained, finally plumping for a far-from-Mexican Sweet Manhattan. Red Vermouth, Scotch, Angostura Bitters, blended to perfection in his upturned bobby's helmet. As he applied the finishing touches the olive was suddenly plucked from his hand. He looked about him. Swifts, hundreds of them, just back from Africa and starved by a 4 thousand mile flight, now strafing him in a frenzy of darting beaks. Snaith rammed a single olive up his nose then flicked out the rest of the packet and the birds scattered down in pursuit. He pressed a finger over his empty nostril and with a grunt the bitter fruit shot forth, the cocktail plipping as it broke the surface. Downing it with a single gulp he sensed they would be back.

An hour later, somewhere near Yeovil, he passed the late Mrs Henderson twitching and crackling on the wires of a pylon. Later still came Dartmoor. Boys on a crag threw stones; they were but ants to Snaith. Ants in short trousers. Hardly rivals to the hungry birds he sensed still lingered. As the sun beat on his face he drifted in and out of sleep, rousing at dusk sticky-mouthed, escaping dreams of pursuit by a giant bee.

*Thppppzzzzzz-zzzzzz-zzzzzzz-zzzz!*

Snaith's eyes narrowed – though the vision had stopped the buzzing continued. Craning his neck he saw the Microlight head in from the east, and through bleary stinging eyes made out the face of the missing Detective Sergeant. He was alive! Sing Hosannas! No. It wasn't possible. Snaith knew he must be dreaming. Right up until the bullet whizzed past his chest.

The grizzled gumshoe saw it all now. And what hurt wasn't the betrayal, or knowing Eunice wanted him dead. It was that he hadn't seen the clues. Snaith made out metalwork glinting in the evening sun. A barrel. It was all falling into place - surely the self-same rifle that had gone missing from the umbrella stand in the station canteen.

*'She's using you you fool'*, he cried.

*'We're in love...'* bellowed back the lad.

*'Love!?! She can't love, she doesn't know how...'* Snaith screamed above the whirr of the ever-nearing blades.

*'We're going to travel the world'* yelled the Detective Sergeant, *'on my copper's life insurance...'*

So that was it. Before helping him fake his own death Eunice had wormed her way not just into the DS's heart, but also into his generous Home Office Remuneration Package. And that wasn't all. Snaith suddenly remembered his own life policy, still active, Eunice the sole beneficiary. He'd thought it strange when she'd insisted he take one out on the steps of the divorce court. Yes, she'd known all along how this would pan out... that he'd be the first to volunteer to follow in the boy's footsteps.

*'You fool...'* roared Snaith, *'She'll break your heart then stamp on the pieces. Just like she did with me'.*

But the boy was now a stranger to the land of reason. Eunice had done it again. Played them both, played them like a cheap accordion. It had all been worked out, down to her yanking off Snaith's Kevlar reinforced trousers to reveal a bigger target.

The Microlight sputtered ever nearer, now just yards away. The DS raised the gun. If you've never stared down the barrel of a gun, it's impossible to describe the sensation. It's a rush, a buzz... imagine the rich flood of adrenaline that comes when your card's refused in Sainsburys. In front of a queue. Maybe one with a vicar in it. Well it's two, possibly even three times as intense as that.

## Crack!

The lad failed to account for recoil and Snaith felt the bullet part his hair as the tiny craft shook like Presley's hips. The boy knew what he was doing though. Hit the man not the balloon, then the evidence will be lost at sea. Snaith rammed his hands down into his pockets. Ham rolls. Nothing but damn canteen ham rolls for the journey. Well, if there was ever a day for dead meat. A shot rang past, Snaith's left sock suspender gave out. If the next one missed it wouldn't even matter, the lovesick DS could just smack him on the temple with the fat end of the gun.

Then… a swift darted past. Then another. And more still! Swooping about the rolls in his hand like electrons in an atom, albeit an entirely diagrammatic one. Suddenly Snaith knew what he must do, yanking roll upon roll from his pockets and shredding them to create a tumbling Hovis snowstorm.

The gun was now just a foot from his temple… Snaith could see the lad's eye through the sight as the blizzard of crumbs sucked back toward the propeller. In a split second the birds were at the bread, among the blades. Feathers, blood, graunching, flames – and the tiny craft tumbled to the ground.

Snaith, now a dozen rolls and a bladder-full lighter

felt the slackening of gravity's embrace and gently rose, goose-bumps forming Braille on his legs as the sun ducked behind the horizon.

SOMEWHERE IN THE NORTH ATLANTIC.
2:14 pm.
Detective Inspector Snaith woke to the sound of sobbing and his eyes slowly came to focus on the back of the tatty kagoul.

'Look. There's no need for all this', he croaked.

'Have to do it solo...' The man's mumbled reply was almost lost on the breeze. 'If I get there with you in the boat it'll all have been for nothing. *Nothing*'.

At that the Yachtsman turned and with immense effort raised the dead turtle high above his head.

'So sorry... but solo, must be solo'.

Snaith could just make out his smeared reflection in the surface of the hard shell above: weak, tiny, cowering. With the last of his strength he hedgehogged in preparation for the blow.

*Thruddahump!*

The sound came but he felt nothing. Lifting a timid lid he saw the black boom flick back and forth across the sun, and then saw the body it had broken now lying at his feet.

★

Snaith eyed the mess inside the cabin: burnt out radio, empty tins, shredded maps. He pulled the life raft from its housing - A yank and a hiss then he wrestled the swelling orange blob over the rail. Slamming the head of the anchor into the deck he was in no doubt that what he was doing was right: The Gaffer had stressed this Op was covert. Code Red. Besides, if he stuck around with the body he could see another ocean, larger than this, stretching as far as the horizon and beyond. One of paperwork.

The Atlantic switched from inky black to blue as it fountained through the split hull. Snaith mustered all his strength and leapt from one craft to the other. He didn't see the mast tip drop beneath the ocean's surface, he had long since lost consciousness – his tiny raft a tray, the sea beneath a drunken waiter's hand.

## CASE CLOSED

## POST SCRIPT

DI Snaith was picked up a day and a half later by the cruise ship 'The Manatee'. After 24 hours rehydration he spent the fortnight till it docked at Southampton belting out numbers in its Copacabana ballroom. Three shows a day, four at weekends.

# IN PLOD WE TRUST

*'Maybe crime doesn't pay...*
*but the perks sure are sweet'*

## AUTHOR'S NOTE

Mr Evans believes this may well be, chronologically, the first of these cases. He suspects that, due to it's highly confessional nature, the Detective delayed its telling until he felt a mutual trust had been established.

## SCOTLAND YARD. PRINCESS ANNE GYMNASIUM. FRIDAY 8:24am.

'You're pushing them too hard Snaith', barked the Gaffer surveying the cavernous space chock-full of elderly ladies beavering away at trays on their laps. 'Too damn hard'.

Detective Inspector Snaith turned briskly on his heel; just a little too fast, performing a full 360 degree turn rather than the proposed 180 – his dramatic exit becoming a pirouette. Luckily the Gaffer hadn't seen, too busy chewing fingernails. These days half the station budget seemed to go on fingernails.

'Goddammit Snaith, we need results', roared the Gaffer. 'Results!' he yapped, at such a volume that half the old dears looked up, and two genuflected.

'And that's what you're going to get' muttered Snaith, backing out slowly so as to avoid any more problems with heel spins – he could always perfect those at home.

The disconsolate detective trudged through the herd of scrotum-skinned nanas arthritically fingering duplicate jigsaw pieces and once more cursed the butcher who had forced his hand. For the umpteenth time he poked and prodded the bare bones of the case. It's a well-known fact that every single serial killer, without exception, leaves an enigmatic clue somewhere about their victim. A page from a Victorian Storybook, the chrysalis of an insect, or perhaps something a bit less subtle, like another body.

And this guy certainly wasn't the exception to prove that rule. He proved it by obeying it, just like almost all the rest. And his twisted gifts... were single jigsaw pieces.

It was a case that had taunted the Force for yonks, just a month after Snaith's first day had come murder number one. Now the tally stood at 298.

Snaith looked about the aisles at the Tessellation Squad. A Tessellation Squad – what could he have been thinking? Or was it genius? Only time would tell. But for now there was only one fact that would forever remain unchanged – police work doesn't run on excuses... or method, or evidence. It runs on Je Ne Sais Quoi, Va Va Voom, Spark, Flicker, Brio, Élan, Panache: The indefinable 7 dwarves of hunch that must get the Snow White of deduction up the duff so she can birth an arrest. Everyone knew that, it was page one of the manual.

SQUAD MEETING ROOM. SHORTLY AFTER.
They were them. The Squad. Converged for another crisis meeting. When push came to shove they were never found wanting. When those that couldn't stand the heat got out of the kitchen these guys just climbed in the oven. Or at very least put their hands under the grill. And so they sat, equally spaced round the perimeter of the table, easily the most practical arrangement. Previous attempts at 'stacking' having caused one or two problems with status.

Detective Inspectors Snaith, Wilton and Harris: Their names said consecutively read like a list.

DI Snaith - Alcoholic Womaniser.

DI Wilton - Womanising Alcoholic.

DI Harris - Workaholic Alcoholic Asthmatic, in his condition Womanising just wasn't an option.

Snaith sprung an aspirin from its plastic prison, Harris yanked yet more Ventolin down into his bagpipe lungs. Then there was Wilton, the maverick with a fondness for the plastic surgeon's scalpel. The sort of man who would barge into the interrogation room, then, just to intimidate a suspect, puff up his throat to the size of a beach ball or slide his tongue out between his lips and waggle the little bell he'd attached to the end.

Snaith put a cup to his lips. Since the day ex wife Eunice had left he'd taken his coffee black. It reminded him of her heart. The colour of her heart. Not the flavour... coffee could never be that bitter. He looked around him at the steely coppers, tin stars in an ever-expanding universe of crime. Still, better here than at home. Everywhere he looked in the flat he still saw her face. That novelty wallpaper had been a big mistake. Eunice. One hell of a woman: if only he'd let her know what he'd felt for her, if only he'd been able to leave his work at the station, if only he'd not held her out of the window by her ankles that time. Well, those times. Dammit, a man had to let of steam somehow. Eunice... he'd called her Rusty, as she'd always bought her underwired bras from the Pound Shop.

Suddenly the door swung open, stamping on the brakes of Snaith's drive down memory lane. They had all been waiting for one man, and that man had just walked in.

The Gaffer: Chocoholic - evidence of his dark (and milk) secret dotted about a collar as taughtly stretched as the resources that kept the metropolis just the decent side of anarchy. The Gaffer. Shriveled as a care home fruit bowl. A man with his past behind him, his future yet to happen. An alloy of copper... and steel. 90% Holmes, 10% Watson, 100% Bastard. A 'bottle-of-Scotch-in-the-filing-cabinet' kind of guy smoking 80 a day through every available orifice.

'So gentlemen', he rasped with a voice as rough as the plastering in a country pub. 'Another murder, another piece of a jigsaw. The way I see it we've just got to put together the pieces of this jigsaw, and we'll solve it'.

'That's what you say about every case Guv', chipped in DI Wilton.

'Maybe, but usually it's an attempt to describe the deductive process using an abstract turn of phrase... and this time, well, I just mean it literally'.

DI Harris was next to grill the head honcho.

'So it's a simile?'

'No' replied the Gaffer. 'If it were a simile I'd have

said the crime was *like* a jigsaw'.

'So is it a metaphor then?' probed Wilton. 'Because you said the case is a jigsaw'.

'I don't think so' answered the Gaffer. 'Because a metaphor is still a comparative literary device, whereas this case is actually a jigsaw'.

At last, they were making progress.

## ALPHA PANDA. FRIDAY 11:17am

DI Snaith drove to clear his mind, banging his hand hard on the wheel in time to the music, pedestrians shooting irritated scowls with every short beep of the horn. Driving sharpened his mind, it had always been so. Even during his eighteen-month ban he'd solved at least two murders wedged in the bright red plastic postman's van outside ASDA as it rocked to a primeval rhythm, spurred on to smoking point as he'd thrust in one coin after another. His expenses claim that month had whipped up one hell of a shitstorm.

The wipers flicked the drops from the windscreen, lashing out like a woman spurned in love. The troubled detective screeched to halt, wrestled momentarily with his demons, lost yet again and tore open the glove compartment. Goddammit he needed a drink. Gin, lemon juice, sugar, soda, cherries, dammit, where was the orange zest? He couldn't mix a Tom Collins without orange zest. He may be a bastard, but he wasn't a monster.

The radio crackled, more bad news. Snaith spied a

bumper sticker on a passing car – Shit Happens.

'Tell me about it' he muttered.

WASTE GROUND. NOON.

DI Snaith strode past scrubby grass that waved from splits in tarmac bubbled like the crust of a crème brule. Then, when he was sure he had the attention of the Constables guarding the crime scene, he vaulted the barrier of crime tape with his trademarked Fosbury Flop.[3]

In front of him lay another corpse, yet he felt nothing. He'd seen too many: at murder scenes, mortuaries, over-exuberant interrogation sessions.

Snaith shot a look to the ashen-faced young PC who

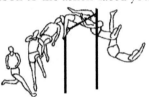

Stages of the Fosbury Flop

---

[3] *DI Snaith's tape-crossing technique the 'Fosbury Flop' was pioneered by High Jump gold medalist Dick Fosbury at the 1968 Mexico Olympic. It involves clearing the bar as illustrated overleaf, and has revolutionized both that event and British police procedure.*

stood nervously fingering his helmet. His eyebrows demanded explanation… fluttering about his temple like moths round a candle, singeing their wings in a seemingly illogical frenzy of genetic programming. They were very complex eyebrows. Yet wasn't every policeman a moth? Which of them could honestly say they'd never mistaken a burning flame for the cool glow of the moon? Snaith certainly had. About 4 times.

So, the pace had upped. Another murder, and only a week since the killer had last struck, strangling a middle-aged dentist with his own belt before filling his pockets with gravel and hoofing him into the Thames.

Snaith knew the answer to his question before he even asked it, but he asked it anyway, just to maintain belief in his own predictive abilities.

'Jigsaw piece in the pocket?'

The PC nodded and held aloft an evidence bag, the little piece of card inside once more tying the thin blue line in knots.


BACK AT THE SQUAD HQ. SATURDAY 1:47am

Another crisis meeting. The Gaffer slapped a buff file down onto the tabletop, grubby as tinker's mattress, dog-eared as a puppy's head: The Profile. It was all they had left.

'For what it's worth', he mumbled, 'We know the killer's either Caucasian or non Caucasian, of indefinite gender, and has a possible age'.

'Of...?' Probed Harris.

'It just says he has a possible age' sighed the Gaffer. 'The only thing it states for sure is... is that he's Aries. Or Capricorn, but with Sagittarius rising'.

Wilton prodded the folder with one of his steel paws.

'The way I see it we only know two things about him for certain. He's a bastard. But he's a clever bastard'.

DI Snaith knew Wilton was wide of the mark. Knew because he was the only one amongst them who could see things from the killer's point of view. As he too had taken a life. That of the woman who had given life to him. But as Snaith had lifted the pillow from her newly frozen features he'd consoled himself that it had been a mercy killing. Mum had been in great pain. Well, certainly since the previous week when he'd 'helped' her down the stairs.

'Snaith!'

The Gaffer's scornful bark yanked the Detective back to the moment.

'...if those old biddies don't pull something out of the hat in the next two days I'm sending them all back to Worthing'.

'But...'

The Gaffer shot Snaith a look that could only mean one of many things.

'Really? A tessellation squad. What were you thinking man? I thought I'd seen it all. Coppers mixed up with brasses, pigs caught with their fingers in the till...'

'Gaffer's paying their wives to do criminal profiles', muttered Snaith.

'You leave Alice out of this! She does her best. Dammit, she had you down as Libra after only 4 guesses!'

Wilton and Harris looked down at their shoes.

'Libra the bastard', spat the Gaffer. He yanked 4 cigarettes from the bucket by his desk, swallowed one and lit the remaining 3.

'Two days Snaith, then it's Wilton's case'.

'Right you are Guv' croaked Snaith, his voice now weak as Women's Royal Voluntary Service coffee.

The dejected Detective squeaked back his chair and made for the door, eyes now damp as a lavatory carpet.


SATURDAY 4:42am

Snaith nestled in the straw beneath his desk. No time to go home, besides, what was the point? There was no warm welcome, just microwave meals and memories of Eunice. The Gaffer appeared at the doorway.

'The old ladies... you were right. They've finally got something'.

As Snaith pulled on his socks he wondered whether this was just another false dawn, like when they'd stared at the completed jigsaw just a month before, the folly of his conclusion then still ringed in his ears.

'So... We're looking for a kitten. Possibly two'. The pathology reports just didn't scan. The victims had met their end by strangulations. No small scratches, no fleabites. Besides, the chances of such a young cat throttling so many adult males was hard to believe. Especially after the police artist had knocked up that sketch.

Following that debacle the old ladies had been frisked on arrival each morning to stop them bringing in their own puzzles. The Force wasn't prepared to take a beating from the Press on this one, and if that meant the daily strip-search of 45 octogenarians, then so be it.

But there it seemed to be, spread out on the floor in front of them. A classic landscape format school photograph: Aylesbury Boys Comprehensive. Snaith shuddered. His school, his final year, the picture complete, but for only two absent faces. It was suddenly clear - Each and every pupil from the photo slain, with the piece bearing the next victim's face concealed about the cadaver.

The Gaffer was the first to break the silence.

'Let's keep this under our hats lads, it's probably the sort of link we should've picked up on sooner'. Snaith shuddered, knowing his face was one that occupied, or more accurately failed to occupy one of the two remaining gaps.

'All of them. Same school, same year', snarled the

Gaffer. 'Any theories gentlemen?'

'Coincidence?' ventured Wilton.

Suddenly the door swung open and in ran a breathless young P.C.

'About bloody time', bellowed the Gaffer, 'I've been waiting hours for those fingernails'.

But the lad said nothing, just dropping a blood-soaked jigsaw piece down in front of them. So, this was it. Now only one face still missing. And it was the face of Detective Inspector Snaith. Snaith's head span, surely this could mean only one thing. He *must* be the killer. Up till that moment he'd considered his Cocktail-induced blackouts little more than holidays from reality. Brief oblivions from which he'd wake sticky-eyed in railway sidings, scrapyards or woodland. Almost like a hobby. Could it be that at the same time as solving crime he'd actually been committing it? As this frightful revelation overwhelmed him Snaith prayed that his 'murders solved' exceeded his 'murders done'. At least then, if only statistically, he would still have been an asset to the Force.

But before he could sweep up the pieces of yet another cracked case a terrible realisation overwhelmed him. According to the photograph there was still one more murder he, the killer, had yet to perform. That of the boy still missing from the jigsaw. That of Snaith himself.

Suddenly Snaith felt his hands slide up his shoulders, he felt his fingers tighten round his throat; he felt his thumbs press into his windpipe as he wrestled against himself to save his very life...

*'Uggluuuughrhhh! Archhhhhhggglllillllurghhhh!'*

4:47am

Snaith came to, midway through the most brutal of Gaffer-slappings, his cheeks burning fierce as a boy scout's bonfire. Pulling up his trousers he got to his feet and threw his superior a look that demanded verbal feedback in the form of words conveying meaning.

'It wasn't you you idiot' growled the big man. 'We've got CCTV footage showing you were across town at the time of death'.

'Thank God', hissed Snaith.

The Gaffer pressed a remote and Snaith shrunk in his chair as he watched grainy footage of his grubby form dancing naked in a shopping centre water feature. He suddenly knew it was time for the blackouts to stop, and, burying face in hands vowed to ease up on the Manhattans.

'None before lunch' he mumbled.

Suddenly Wilton stopped chewing on the tip of his tail and looked up.

'We've been looking for the pieces all this time', he began with sage authority, 'but maybe... just maybe, we should have been looking... for the box.'

The men turned as one to face the Body-Dismorphic-Disordered Detective, hungry for further insight. But it wasn't forthcoming, Wilton just looking around sheepishly before returning to nibbling his latest surgical addition.

Snaith crawled to the all-but-complete tableaux still taunting them from the office floor and a wry smile began to play about his lips.

'Get me a Panda'[4], he choked.

6:02am

'What took you?' croaked the old man.

Snaith looked about the dim room. Carriage clock, sausage dog draft excluder, a TV remote mummified in yellowing tape. Could this really be the lair of a killer?

'Well… OK', he continued, 'So I may be a bad man, but I was a damn good Headmaster'.

Snaith's nostrils caught the acrid smell of smoke coiling up from the old man's pipe, and his mind turned to thoughts of ex wife Eunice. No… no time for flashbacks now… he must remain focused.

'So Detective' coughed the ex Head, jiggling the oxygen cylinder that supplied his nose pipe, as though it was in some way to blame for his wheezing rather than the tobacco. 'How did you work it out?'

Snaith's mind replayed the intricate thrusts and

---

[4] *UK slang for a small or medium sized marked police car*

parries of his deductive process.

'Well... Apart from me, you were the only one in that photo who was still alive'.

'Not for much longer', croaked the smoking remains that sat before him. 'Not for much longer........ Son!'

Snaith's brow furrowed.

'Yes. You are the errant fruit of my once vivid loins'.

Snaith's eyes narrowed.

'To be honest I thought you'd have worked it out and come for me years ago. Maybe after I'd done just two or three. I only really meant to 'do in' the boys who bullied you. Then, well, when you failed to show I kept going, and I suppose... I just got a taste for it'.

Snaith slowly shook his head, something didn't make sense. But then the old man solved the puzzle.

'Well, not the last dozen or so. Look at the state of me. I subcontracted them out – that Head Teacher's pension's surprisingly generous you know'.

The DI felt for the cocktail parasol in permanent residence in his breast pocket, and pushed a thumb down hard on the pointy end to block the memories of his childhood that forever bubbled beneath the brittle crust of his sanity.

'Your mother. A dinner lady at the school, you remember. Well, let's just say she may have been a good mother –'

Snaith shrugged.

'- but she was quite a bad woman'.

The procession of 'Uncles' that had blighted Snaith's formative years once more began their menacing shuffle past his mind's eye: 'Uncle' Michael, who'd made him ride dogs round the car park of The George while the regulars threw coins... 'Uncle' Frank, who'd taken his mother to Malta for 10 Days, leaving the infant detective home alone with nothing but a washing-up bowl full of corned beef and a pile of broken biscuits...

'I've been waiting decades for you to come. Years kept alive by this accursed machine. Turn it on would you? I think we're missing Bargain Hunt'.

Snaith stared at the murderous husk as it jabbed the remote control. He'd never take the stress of court, let alone sharing a cell with some knuckle-dragging Asbo-magnet grappling with his John Thomas in the bunk above. At last Snaith understood the root of his brutal psyche. With eyes now moist as a Labrador's nose he leaned slowly forward and tightened the stopcock on the oxygen cylinder. The old man just gave a nod and slumped back in his chair.

'Goodnight dad', whispered the Detective, before dropping the pipe into the waste paper basket. As the smoke began to rise Snaith slowly shut the door behind him, pausing only to wipe his prints from the knob.

CASE CLOSED

*Tales From the Casebook...*

# THE PASSION OF
# THE SNAITH

*'It is better to have loved and lost...*
*than have been set upon with a hammer.*
*But only just'.*

## OFFICIAL SECRETS ACT

In order to conform to the United Kingdom Official Secrets Act (1989) this document has been subject to redaction by Her Majesty's Home Office.

GOODSTOCK FESTIVAL. FIELDS NEAR
███████. ██████-DAY HOLIDAY WEEKEND.

'All we know for sure is he's a sick bastard', wheezed the Gaffer, pushing his head through the tent flaps to cough up yet another 'gold watch', the ground outside now resembling the aftermath of a food fight in an oyster bar.

The Squad were far from their usual patch, assisting a Midlands murder enquiry. 9 dead, the Perp had been christened 'The Cuddler' as they'd left torsos crushed by embraces of truly ursine excess. Detective Inspector Snaith could still picture the autopsy photos - it was like winklepicker ribs had played keepy-ups with melon lungs.

Snaith surveyed the tent's interior: The Gaffer's buttocks jiggled as he retched to clear his lungs, DI Wilton's whiskers twitched as he dozed in his basket, DI Harris went at his eczema like a widow at a Scratchcard.

The Squad were clearly no boy scouts. They'd been given this weekend as a break, downtime, R&R. They were in the area anyway so why not? Snaith flumped down onto his sleeping bag. Most men his age might resent the privations of camping, for him it made a pleasant change. Sundays usually saw him flat-out and staring at the ceiling, the searing heat from a Fray Bentos Steak Pie held back by a SWAT team Kevlar vest. He'd once woken up blind, only to find he'd rolled over during a nap and wedged his face in the empty tin.

The tarnished copper pulled a mirror from his washbag and stared into a small disc of silvered glass fit only for a cockatoo's cage.

'Who's a pretty boy?' he muttered. The answer lay before him in a reflection that struggled to maintain eye contact. It was an eternal spring for the gin blossom; blown capillaries criss-crossed his nostrils like pubes stuck to the soap in a doss-house washroom. His brow furrowed like sand at low tide. Beneath it sat the eyes, bags below fully packed – as though they'd seen too much and wanted out. He lifted a liver lip to reveal chipped teeth, dental Himalayas the colour of urinal cakes. Then crowning it all was the hair. Well, hairs. A meager combover evoking the roof structure of a Norman Foster airport terminal.

*''We-gutt-ta-hinnstawwlll-micraway-vuvvens...'*

Distant croaking from the main stage tugged Snaith back to the moment...

*Schhkruuuhh! Schhhkruuuhh! Schhhkruuuhhh!*

...DI Harris adding a samba beat as he liberated yet more epidermal snow from his largest organ.

*Brrring brriiiiiing!*

Snaith was at his phone faster than a resting actor. A moment's silence, then the line went dead. Number withheld, just like all the other times. Once a month for the past year, though lately it had upped to twice a week. He stumbled from the tent and rubbed his eyes, surveying what had become Europe's largest free festival - every canvas dome and camper van neatly rowed, as though Glastonbury had been annexed by The Daily Express.

It may have been only the forth 'Goodstock' but this D█████a Day weekend more than 80,000 had joined the permanent encampment hunkered down by her graveside, convinced of the good lady's imminent resurrection. Most here thought she still lived, dispensing tenderness incognito. Some were more realistic, and knew she'd been tragically taken, but also knew she'd soon return to tend the needy. Snaith was one of a foolish few, those who thought there'd been a crash, she'd died, and that was that.

Snaith exited The Squad's tent, which compared poorly to the others. Not canvas but tarpaulin and crime tape, last pitched in a wooded glade while inside forensics frisked a bludgeoned aupere for DNA.

Snaith drunk a deep draught of the morning air, choking on the pollen that floated over from acre upon acre of floral tribute. He eyed the sheep that dotted a distant field, then trudged toward the distant stage. Billy Joe-elle, SuperTramp, Will-now-not-quite-so-Young: all happy to play gratis to honour her memory. If only, mused Snaith, that tragic night back in ███████ she could have stayed as firmly in the middle of the road as they had.

This year's immense attendance was surely down to 'The Miracle of Holmes' Place' –

- a track suit top found at a branch of ▮▮▮▮▮'s own Gym chain that appeared to bear a sweat-stain image of her face.

Her devotees were convinced it foretold her imminent reappearance. They, and indeed Ladbrokes, believed the most likely location was Great Ormond Street Hospital for Sick Children – indeed for days now the roads outside had been so rammed with gawpers ambulances had all but given up trying to reach it.

Suddenly the burly Rozzer loosed a tear, recalling his own time spent with the woman who'd touched more hearts than Magdi Yacoub.

NEW SCOTLAND YARD. DALEY THOMPSON CANTEEN. SUMMER 1997.

'Oh come on Guv, it can't be my turn again. It *cant'*.

'Dit dit dit dah dah dit dah dit dit dit daaaah', beeped

the Gaffer's Morsebox, tobacconated tonsils having once more robbed the big man of his voice.

Snaith slapped down his mess tray at the prospect of another week of the dreaded Royal Duties: Twiddling cufflinks while the Queen snipped ribbons, crouching unseen on the carriage floor as it trundled down The Mall, being ridden round the croquet lawn by the visiting King of Tonga. He could do without it.

'Dit Dit Dit Dah'

'Kensington Palace eh?' replied Snaith, verbally raising his eyebrows.

★

They had made love within the hour. At a Polo tournament. Ducking into a Marquee, she dropping to the floor at the mere touch of his hand. Rolling among crested napkins, Snaith's moment of ecstasy heightened when the small wooden ball from the game outside shot under the canvas and wedged fast between his buttocks.

But her charity work came first, and that night he was forced to slap, punch then finally drown his sorrows as her undercarriage left the runway at R.A.F. ███████████ destined for ███████████.

Only hours later Snaith had first met Eunice, in an All-You-Can-Eat Marmite bar on the Strand. They'd gone on to a nightclub, Eunice traversing the floor with a confident swagger, losing her cool only for the briefest moment when she'd slipped on the polo ball that rolled from Snaith's trouser leg.

If only it could have done the same two months later when the vicar had uttered the fateful words,

'Does anyone here present know of any lawful impediment?'

He finally realised he had married Eunice on the rebound.

'Do you Mr Oil take Miss Water... Mr Chalk take Miss Cheese... Mr Crisps take Miss Chewing Gum...'

He'd even missed the first dance with his bride, hiding in the gents playing that final phone message from D███a time and over again.

*'I'm sorry I had to go, but there are orphans here... just so many orphans'.*

GOODSTOCK FESTIVAL.
A FLASHBACK LATER.

*'...got-summ-hinn-stawww-micraway-vuvvens...'*

The croaking Knopfler arthritically fingered strings on the main stage. In old age the body shrinks but the features grow, and there was the man that proved it big time. Open pores sat like seeds in the bulbous strawberry of his nose, his head the body of a butterfly, his ears the wings.

DI Wilton bounded alongside; his history also intertwined with that of the great lady's. Snaith noticed a single tear hanging from a whisker tip. DI Wilton had headed one of the many enquiries into her death. And it had convinced him there had to be more to D████a's end than met the eye. How could she have died in the crash? After all, in his reconstruction the Mercedes driver, two bottles of '76 Burgundy the worse for wear, had ploughed into a taxi queue a full 2km before even reaching the tunnel.

Snaith lobbed a stick and his body-dismorphic-disordered comrade forgot his sorrows and bounded off in pursuit. He idly plucked fluff from his belly button: his mother always told him it was just a bit of his stuffing coming out, like happened with a teddy bear. Then she'd lift him out the bath and put him in the tumble drier. He could still recall the taunts next day at school, in the showers after cross-country, naked, bruised from head to foot like a monochrome leopard.

August the 31st. Two tragic anniversaries: This, and his split from Eunice. Last year he'd commemorated the collapse of his marriage with a trip to their favourite restaurant. Unfortunately so had she. Him defiantly shoveling his 'Meatfeast' through gritted teeth, her flirting like a senile aunt with the waiters, revealing far too much at the salad bar, serving spoon gripped between her toes, showing more leg than a giraffe and the same absence of knickers. Snaith had stomped home and knocked back a coalscuttle full of Banana Daiquiri before burying his face in a box of her old shoes.

### '*...Ru Raydee in Red, ris Rancing wiv meee...*'

The Detective's eyes narrowed as Prisoner 988693 DeBurgh croaked through caged jaws, lashed to his sack barrow, the bastard clearly feasting on what had become his annual crumb of partial freedom. Diabolic DeBurgh - At least in the movies they have the decency to kill their victims before eating them.

D███a and Eunice. They'd both loved this song. In some ways they were so very similar. D███a throwing herself down the stairs. Eunice, throwing Snaith down the stairs. His Ex wife had even borrowed her classic line –

'There were always three people in this marriage'

- though in Eunice's case it was perhaps a tad more literal: Tony, Geoff, or Bob from the off-license snoring next to them on the mattress while Snaith's teeth ground like a purring tiger. He'd preferred Bob. At least he brought Twiglets. And they were both Stoke fans, which helped take the edge off.

A cry went up and Snaith turned his back on the crooning beast to see a rapidly gathering scrum of late-middle-aged-to-elderly biddies in twin-sets-and-pearls. In an instant he was prizing them apart, thrusting ever deeper toward the cause of their post-menopausal consternation. Putting a hand to his face he felt damp drops. Rain? No. It was blood!

The inner circle parted to reveal a figure, hugged in a ball under the frenzied onslaught of sensible shoes.

'That's enough!', Snaith roared and the bitter hags turned as one and trapped him in their gaze.

'He had it coming', hissed a gaunt paper-skinned harridan, 'He brought in *this!*'

She held aloft a camera, the ultimate Goodstock taboo. Could they steal a soul? Who knows, but years ago on that August night in the city of love, in the shadow of the Eiffel Tower, to the sound of the lapping Seine, yes, in ██████████, they had surely stolen a life.

But the ladies' assaults were futile. The press were as present as ever, helicopters (and in one case a Hello!copter) strafing the skies above, bristling with high definition cameras. The moment passed and with a deft flick of the wrist the crone resumed her swinging of the strap, thrashing out her frustration on the poor bastard's ribs. Snaith stumbled backward, the beating sound rose about him, merging with another of a lower pitch, and yet the stage now lay silent. He spun to face the floral fields, and a chill shot through him –

*Bom! Bom! Bom!*

- through tumbling petals he made out the shape of what seemed to be a ghostly raft, a figure sat upon it. As the pollen fog cleared a mattress of flowers emerged, born aloft a torrent of humanity. Atop it sat a mannequin, its modesty preserved by 'The Miracle of Holmes' Place, a blond bob wig buffing the plastic scalp as it jiggled to the rhythmic adulation of her sycophants below. The throng overwhelmed him and to accompany the drumming came the cries of those who clearly sought to be made whole by the omnipotence of her spirit.

'...back hair! I beg you rid me of my back hair!'

'....good snow, good snow at Val Disere.'

'...And Chamonix! I wouldn't ask, but Marcus has already rented the chalet...'

As Snaith spun like a leaf in a stream he saw DI Harris raising his red-raw eczema to the effigy; the wheezing Gaffer baring his chest in a flurry of flying buttons; and DI Wilton, the light dancing about his raised steel paws like summer sun upon the scales of a salmon, the noble pink fish flicking 'mungst the tumbling translucent pearls of a waterfall to dodge the lunge of a ravenous Grizzly.

Snaith realised only too late that the simile had been far too long, and he'd now lost sight of his colleagues.

### *Brrring brriiiiiing!*

He yanked the phone from his pocket but with the scuff of the crowd the handset tumbled to the mud. He dropped to his knees steadying himself by grabbing tufts of grass to become a boulder in the torrent. Shoes crushed his knuckles as he grappled for the device, then suddenly they were gone and he lay staring at the sun as the drumming receded.

He glanced at the screen and this time... this time it

showed a number.

THE BEDSIT ABOVE THE JADE PALACE
TAKEAWAY IN ███████. LATER THAT DAY.
Snaith squinted through the greasy window, rubbing
his aching buttocks – it had taken 2 hours on sheep-
back to bring him to this tatty flat. Let a Copper know
your number and he'll find you. It's just a quick check,
a reverse directory. Consciously or not, that's what
you must have wanted.

*'Baa-aa-aaaaa!'*

In the car park below Mr Yip and his nephew edged
toward the nervous creature with bristled cleavers.
Snaith mused the turn of events.

So. Here she was. Alive after all. He looked about
the room. On a peeling plastic table stood a spread
which would disgrace even a North Korean harvest
festival. The desperate dietary habits of her not-so-
new life laid bare: Pink wafers, broken biscuits, boot
sale bacon. Nonetheless she still had looks that could
turn heads like a Wimbledon final. In the corner a
battered telly framed the crowd now thrashing in the
lake about her bobbing effigy. Snaith made out the
elderly Sir Elton ███████ on the bank, sausage fingers
jabbing the ivories as his buttocks swung each side of
the piano stool like saggy Clackers.

D███████a stared blankly at the screen.

'It was 'uckin' years ago' she hissed, cradling head in

hands. 'What in God's name do I have to do for a bit of anonymity? What is *wrong* with these people?'

Snaith could find no words to answer, so instead he took her hand, and she once more yielded, sliding to the floor like a busted tripod. In but a moment he had fully tumesced, transforming from 'Slough West' to 'Reading'.

*(Like most cops Snaith had served in Traffic, and was versed in a common slang that compared erectile function to exit signs)*

He reached down for the clips on his sock suspenders. 'No', she purred, 'Leave them on'.

There and then they made the tenderest love, Snaith kneeling on two economy Doughnuts to guard against splinters from the bare boards beneath. As their ecstasy heightened two quite literally became one as she clambered into his straining police issue Y Fronts.

★

She lay with her head upon him, a mouse nestling in the straw of his chest hair. A satisfied mouse.

As Mr and Mrs Yip bickered in the shop beneath, on the tiny telly the multitude still flailed in the lake.

Snaith drained his post-coital Manhattan, having had the foresight to wedge the cocktail shaker in his underpants waistband during his final thrusts.

They talked of everything, and nothing. But mainly of stuff about her: Her desperate hunt for anonymity, the years existing on coupons, her reluctant to sign on, uncomfortable with the idea of living off the state. On the screen the telephoto 'copter shots came thick and fast. Snaith thought he made out DI Wilton thrashing about in the water like a wasp-stung toddler.

'You know what that place needs', she whispered. 'A few land mines'. 16 years in the Royal Family - it stood to reason she new her way round a joke.

He looked down at his now exhausted organ. Yes, as a man he was satisfied, but not as a Detective. He must have answers.

'I understand why. But... but how? The House of Winds■, MI■, The ■■■■sian Gendarmerie – you fooled them all'.

She put a finger to his lips.

'If anyone deserves to know it's you'.

Snaith lay dumbstruck as she described a scheme unparalleled, one watertight as Pampers Pull-Ups.

'After ■■■■■■■, I simply ■ and ■■■. That lay the way clear for to ■■■■ but ■■. With that in place it just took a small ■■■ and a pomegranate, and so ■ a

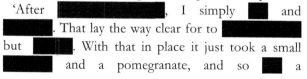

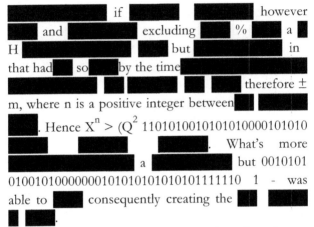

██████████ if ███ ████ however ██ and ████ excluding ██ % ███ a H █████████████ but ██████ in that had ██ so ██ by the time ████ ████████ therefore ± m, where n is a positive integer between ██ ████ ██. Hence $X^n > (Q^2$ 11010100101010100001010 10 ██████ █████ ████████. What's more ████████████████ a ████████ but 0010101 0100101000000010101010101010101111110 1 - was able to ████ consequently creating the ██ ████ █ ██.

No sound came but the gentle ma-thwuck-na-happp of the extractor fan in the shop below. He could but marvel at the mental capacity of the creature that lay spent beside him. Clever mouse.

Snaith shot a glance at her stomach, still flat as an accountant's wedding. He suddenly found he had one more thing to ask. And she seemed to know it.

'The rumours... were you...'

'I, I meant to call. I did call...'

'So - '

'It - '

'The - '

They paused to break the stalemate and Snaith's eyes, newly accustomed to the landlord's 40 Watts hunted the room. Coloured blocks... a bouncy ball. She went once more to speak, but instead of soft tones came the clang of a big shoe on the fire escape below. Suddenly she was on her feet.

'If you ever loved me... go!'

'But...'

'Go... GO! Damn you!'

Her eyes burnt fierce as charcoal briquettes as she stuffed Snaith's clothes down the front of his underpants and pushed him through the door.

'Go. GO! And promise me you'll never return'.

★

The wool scratched like pan scrubbers on Snaith's tired thighs. He shouldn't be surprised, it was natural she should have found another man. Besides, what right had he to want her when that very morning she had been dead to him?

*'Baaaaa-aaa!'*

'Know what you mean' mumbled Snaith to his knock-kneed steed. But what was he saying? He was no sheep. Sheep follow orders; he'd built a career on precisely the opposite. He was going to go back... he had to go back. It was now or never.

40 MINUTES LATER. THE BEDSIT ABOVE
THE JADE PALACE TAKEAWAY.
Snaith stood over her crumpled torso, looking upon the price of his dither. Crushed, or as was now clear 'Hugged' lifeless. He saw her smiling face. She had wanted this, peace at last, the years of loneliness and

91

hiding finally at an end.

Through the bedroom door in the half-light a dungereed oaf dropped a crumpled teddy. The little propeller on his cap span in the breeze from the window as he patted together his fat murderous hands.

Snaith knew those eyes. Sure, they weren't bloodshot, and the hair was thicker, but there could be no denying this was the fruit, or maybe vegetable of his loins. It may have only been the once but it seemed his sperm had battered their way to her egg with a persistence which did credit to his Special Patrol Group training.

Yes, Snaith had chanced upon a son, and at the same time surely found 'The Cuddler'. It was suddenly clear to him - the Gaffer had been way off the mark. These hadn't been crimes of hatred, but ones of affection. But just a bit too much of it. The boy was clearly half D███a, half Snaith. Her unlimited affection for mankind - soured by his excess, his brutal cynicism, his inability to know when to stop.

★

It had been a routine cover up. After all there was no need to worry about witnesses. The entire nation had been glued to their sets to watch the increasingly frenzied festival while the little sheep had staggered for a mile before collapsing by a stream under her dead weight.

Dawn would do the rest. The country was itching for a miracle, was it really so wrong to let them have one? Snaith could already picture the stalls, wheelchair ramps down into the now-Holy water, coach trips, souvenirs... surely all just weeks away.

NEW SCOTLAND YARD. BASEMENT CELLS.
A FORTNIGHT LATER.

The Gaffer slid back the cover to the inspection hole in the cell door. Billy Attle, chief suspect in a South London drug ring wheezed on the concrete floor. His now blue head nodded weakly at his captors. He couldn't take another hug.

'I think someone's ready for their confession', muttered the Gaffer. Not entirely by the book but the Squad's conviction rates had never been higher.

*'Snaith!'*

Detective Inspector Snaith, woodloused in body armour, hands stuffed with wax crayons, nervously approached the cell door. Time to spend some quality time with his boy.

CASE CLOSED

# PAEDO FOXTROT BRAVO!

*'There may be no 'I' in Team...*
*but there is one in Crime. And a 'Me''*

THE PRESS ROOM. NEW SCOTLAND YARD.
9:00 AM

Both parents, eyes rubbed red, stared down the lens for their latest appeal. Before them a bouquet of microphones, surely soon to be caught by the next brides-to-be in some tragic marriage of misfortune and media.

Detective Inspector Snaith sat in the shadows, impassive. These days it took more than a snatched tot to tug his heartstrings. Especially since Earl's Court and the Miss World Pageant. An as-yet unidentified terror group had released a mouse, and the beauty Queens had stampeded. Carnage. To this day he fought back tears when checking the oil in the Panda car – as the bloodstained sash of the late Miss Latvia still served as a replacement fanbelt. At least she hadn't died for nothing. She had died so his battery could remain fully charged.

Snaith studied the wretched couple, in the hope of picking out the metaphorical onion-in-the-hankie. As the mother sobbed like a car trying to start with damp plugs Snaith doubted his own would have even noticed him gone. He could picture her now, down the precinct fishing coins from the water feature before heading for the greyhound track to bellow from the railing, dog after dog leaving her hoarse. Him left with his aunt for days. A bow-fronted woman, mudslide breasts stopped dead on a spacehopper belly. Puffing on butts from the bus station floor while Snaith played at her feet, rummaging through the shoebox of assorted Lego her cat would mistake for its litter tray. Despite this the infant Detective felt safe in her care, beguiled by the light that danced about the crystals of Sambuca which trimmed her moustache, while she wrestled bawdy songs from a battered squeezebox, hoiking grollies into a two-into-one slipper commandeered for a spittoon. Happy days.

The newly childless couple sat spent, faces blotchy-red as thighs on a hen night. Standard police procedure was to move in now and slap the bracelets straight on the pair of them. It had proved around 80% effective. But Snaith sensed these two were different, no clues thus far. No witnesses, DNA, nothing. Only a public hungry for justice. And pictures of it. He turned to DI Wilton.

'Well?'

'Huh?' replied his body dismorphic colleague.

Snaith revolved a finger and Wilton dutifully turned his back. He eyed the raw stitchery either side of his fellow detective's head. Reversed ears. The man never ceased shuffling the cards Mother Nature had dealt him. Granted he'd not be surprised from behind but this latest upgrade was clearly not without its drawbacks.

'Those two. Mr and Mrs "Boo-Hoo". We going in?'

'Which two?' said Wilton, staring blankly at the back wall.

EIGHT DAYS LATER. ALPHA PANDA. 2:46pm

'This'll be going live on the website', barked Bob Vernon, the latest headhunted hack to make a big splash at *The Oomph!* Newsgroup. 'So you might want to run a comb through that thing that's squatting on your top lip'.

Snaith's fingernails pierced the steering wheel cover.

'Turn down that one then take the second left...'

The indicator stalk snapped in his hand like a breadstick.

'...not here you idiot - *there*'.

The bonnet nodded as Snaith stamped the brake.

*'I am not an 'uckin' cab!'* he growled.

'Course not mate. Course not. After all... you're free'.


THE SQUAD H.Q. TWO DAYS BEFORE THAT.

*'Look lads, my hands are tied'*, bellowed the Gaffer, sheltering from the lashing rain beneath a desk perched on the fire escape. Despite tumbling stationery and sparks from his monitor, the smoking in the workplace ban still made this the most acceptable compromise.

*'We're skint'*, the big man yelled through the rattling blinds. *'Flat broke. Potless. Borassic'*.

Snaith pinched the bridge of his nose; this funding crisis depressed him like raisins trodden into a new carpet.

*'We've already blown twice our annual budget'*. The Gaffer

threw DI Wilton a look as dirty as a bumpkin's collar. It hadn't really been Wilton's fault. Previous abductions had prompted 'Have you seen this child' posters. He'd just gone one step further and issued 25,000 'Have you seen this baby' dolls, carbon copies of the snatched infant. At first it seemed a masterstroke - The phones rung red-hot. However further inquiries revealed they were all sightings of the dolls themselves. There were also the 6 people holding them, beaten to human soup by crowds bent on righteous justice. Nasty business. The body-dysmorphic-disordered DI pulled yet another 'oops' face for his boss then rummaged forlornly in his tummy-pouch for a mint.

'Maybe I – '

*'No Harris. You know it's not safe'.*

Poor DI Harris. The hessian head-cover to conceal his pixilated features, combined with eczema, asthma, and spectacle lenses thick as the viewing window in a dolphinarium meant he couldn't risk leaving the station during daylight hours. With the public so Paedo-hungry his unfortunate appearance would surely squeeze their hair trigger. A sudden gust flung the Gaffer's 'world's best gaffer' mug down the steel steps.

*'Look. I'm not happy about it either, but it's the only money on the table. We take this deal... or it's the end of us'.*

The detectives traded doubtful glances.

*'Just work with them. Give them what they need. Snaith, I'm*

*pairing you up with the main one. Vernon. Bob Vernon, Story Editor. For the sake of the Squad... just keep him happy'.*

So there it was. The elite of UK Crime fighting reduced to taking media kick-backs for exclusive first access to the case. *The Oomph!* Newsgroup: page upon page of celebrity tittle-tattle, scaremongery and jingoistic finger-pointing: The public loved it. The circulation-busting Red Top was its historic flagship, leading a fleet of websites, cable channels and a recently launched breast-heavy newsreel embraced by the nation's Multiplexes.

BACK IN ALPHA PANDA. 2:48pm

Vernon briskly turned away from his phone.

'Hey. Dick Tracey. Chop chop! You're not getting paid to have flashbacks'.

The Panda kissed another pothole as they bounced through London's fast growing but untrimmed fringes. It was still London, but London... Beyond The Postcode. Three words that evoked fear, sympathy, curiosity. Since the planning riots a decade before when the capital's bulging belly had finally bust the buckle on the Greenbelt, unregulated construction here had spread like crabs in a barracks.

The city had tumbled outward in huge swathes of ad hoc developments, from shantytown and prefabricated flats to mock Tudor-bethan villa. Off the tarmacked main arteries, the veins and capillaries were axle-snapping moonscapes, power and sanitation dependent on the beneficence of the nearest speculator, till eventually waves of tatty shacks broke on the M25's hard shoulder. The commuter crawl from Clacket Lane services to South Mimms revealed countless tragic vignettes of those who'd failed to grasp the lowest rung of the housing ladder. They were not bad people; indeed many would clamber about the traffic when it jammed, offering bowls of their family meal, grateful for a handful of Credits.

Vernon lobbed a pasty crust out the window and in his rear view mirror Snaith saw feral kids in grubby vests fight foxes for the morsel. Swinging the Panda down a side street he stamped the brakes to dodge a troop of mortgage defaulters, regimented by the pressure of credit, fighting hand-to-hand with Building Society Militia. Half an hour later they still bounced about among the ruts.

'We're wasting time. The kid's not here', muttered Snaith, raising his window.

'Bit too rough for you is it?' chuckled Vernon. 'Maybe you're right, I've not seen a cop since we came in'.

As the window sealed shut Snaith raised a buttock and loosed a noiseless fart. The man was an idiot. There may not be deerstalkers and magnifying glasses but this place was veined like Roquefort cheese with thin blue lines.

'Face it Poirot, the tot's got to be here. This place is crawling with low-life'.

Sure, Snaith knew it wasn't Shangri-La. Only last month he'd busted a human cheese operation. Single mothers, children taken into care by The State so they could be abused through the proper channels, were being milked for what they now had spare for a paltry 2 Credits a litre. But they were still people, good folk in the main, and what's more it was a hell of a place to spend a weekend.

'Stop! Look. Over there!' yapped Vernon.

'Huh?'

'Those Lock Ups. I'll set up on the left near that van, you back up a bit then floor it. I'll catch you on the camera when you screech up'.

'I don't follow'.

'Wallop, out you get' barked Vernon, 'kick in the door, it's live'. He screwed the transmitter onto his camera and barked at his OffissLink. *'Debbie. We're going for a raid'.*

'But it's just a lock up. It's not like the kid's actually *in* there is it?'

'Ah, but we don't know they're *not* in there do we? You want to be a bit more 'glass half full', there's a tiny child's life at stake here mate. I'll bip you when I'm ready for a take – give me your number'.

Snaith fumbled for his phone. He despised the device. The countless functions seemed to nag him like ex wife Eunice. Cameras demanding hilarious shots to send back to people he half-knew who'd sent him pictures of people he quarter-knew gurning drunk at the lens; the music player plagued him with unasked-for tracks of teen studs extolling technique and prowess... some days the damn thing would 'ping!' like a double decker bus full of schoolkids. He remembered the old days – when cops had proper pocket-sized things to give pleasure: Cigarettes, quarter bottles of Scotch, and yes, why deny it, his now semi-retired whang. And to be honest thought Snaith, if anything could use an upgrade...

'Give it here, I'll do it...' muttered Vernon.

...when were they going to put something on it relevant to him? Never mind streaming movies, what about a nasal hair trimmer? The slam of the door roused Snaith from his musings.

'Wakey wakey Columbo'

'You've done that one already' snapped Snaith.

'Remember' said Vernon clicking his fingers, 'wait for my bip, then pedal to the metal.'

Snaith flattened caterpillar eyebrows with a moistened finger, then a moment later came the signal and he obediently crunched the Panda into reverse.

NEW EALING, BEYOND THE POSTCODE.
THAT EVENING.

DI Snaith took a slug from the chipped cup and winced. In place of fresh mint were nettles. Some Mojito! Nonetheless the homemade spirit muffled the frustration of yet another day faux–searching, kicking in random doors while Vernon streamed endless footage back to the *Oomph!*, improvising non stop copy on his eternally active speakerphone, pausing only to draw quick breaths and bellow directions at his pet detective.

Snaith eyed the dim surrounds of Tots Gentlemen's Club, a micro-barn of construction off-cuts held together by cable ties, inertia and optimism. On the stage – a garage door raised at each corner by a milk crate – the stripper gyrated her hips to the incessant techno like a middle-aged nurse well-behind on the rent. Not surprising as that's exactly what she was. The music died and the greasy clientele lifted hands from laps to clap like shitting cows. The cellulite siren tottered across the door, tripped on the handle and stumbled through a curtain. Vernon clicked his fingers and another label-less bottle appeared at the table.

'I know it's hard mate. It's a grim case', he said, topping up their mugs. 'Got one the same age myself'.

Snaith shook his head, a little too visibly.

'Relax. You're not going to get the old 'picture in the wallet' treatment. What's the point? They all look the 'uckin' same at that age don't they?'

Snaith drained his mug.

'Hey, and don't go feeling sorry for our aupere. As long as she's on a camp bed in our attic she's not living back round here somewhere. Or doing *that*'. Vernon flicked a coin at the stretch-marked stripper as she remounted her garage door.

'And what about its mother', said Snaith, raising his

voice against the resuming Eurobeats. 'Your partner?'

'Ah. The delightful Melanie. Think yourself lucky you got me not her mate. She works for the *Oomph!* Too'.

## BETA PANDA. PACO RABANE ESTATE, LUTON. THAT SAME MOMENT.

'It's just some guy though', pleaded DI Wilton as a Johnny Raincoat pushed open the communal door to some flats.

'You can see what he's like'. Melanie Vernon was already assembling her mic. 'You heard what those two said didn't you?'

'Come *on*. They're just nosy old cows who don't like the look of him'.

'You might be prepared to take that risk detective, but there's a tiny child's life at stake here'.

Wilton leant across and whacked her door lock down with a paw.

'You know what it's like round here. Do this and his flat'll be burnt out by breakfast'.

'Let's not forget who's boss here' she spat. 'I only have to make the call and you're back at Hendon in a padded suit getting chased by Alsatians'.

At that she upped the lock, barked 'testing testing' into her lapel mic and was gone. As she reached the piss-stained stairwell a small crowd was already beginning to gather. DI Wilton sunk low in his seat and nibbled fretfully on the tip of his tail.

BACK AT TOT'S GENTLEMEN'S CLUB.
NEW EALING.

At the sound of a distant growl the bouncer thrashed a hand bell and the crowd as one covered ears with sweaty palms. The 21:58 Boston-Heathrow passed overhead on its final approach and the shack shivered like Shackleton.

A moment's silence, the 'all clear' rang and once more tin foil and shoelace nipple tassels resumed their jiggling, the dancer's expression now one of clear relief. Understandably. Only the previous week a frozen Nigerian refugee had tumbled from a lowering undercarriage and bounced down a nearby street like a Barnes Wallace bomb, finally embedding himself in a makeshift casino. 4 Dead.

The bouncer clanged the bell for the 22:01 Singapore-Heathrow and Snaith's chair scraped back, howling like a Wookie at the approaching roar.

'I'm off'.

'Do I have to remind you who's paying your wages?'

Snaith took not so much a deep breath as a sigh in reverse.

'*May* I go? Bob... please'.

'Sure. You've been a good lad today. I'll cab it, as you keep saying this neck of the woods isn't nearly as bad as we print it is'.

As the jet's growl grew the Journo stuffed a note into Snaith's trouser pocket and yelled –

*'Tomorrow, 10 a.m. We'll do a load more raids!'*

Heading for the door Snaith glimpsed the stripper through a tear in the curtain. Breastfeeding. He pulled his hand from his pocket – Bob had given him a crisp Fifty. She could surely use it. But instead Snaith gave it to the bollard-necked bouncer, whispered in his ear then nodded toward Bob Vernon.

SNAITH'S PLACE. 2:42am

The door clicked behind the beleaguered lawman. The flat: 15 years and he still couldn't seem to get Ex wife Eunice out of the place. It didn't help that she'd never returned her key. Every so often she'd make copies and hand them out to strangers. Along with a map. Many was the time he'd returned home to find a gentleman of the road face down on his bed, another Goldilocks low on meds. Snaith could always have changed the locks, but in a way he was glad. It was company. Sometimes, on the off-chance he'd even leave out bowls of Twiglets.

He glanced in at Eunice's sewing room, left just the way it was the day she'd moved out. 'Up Yours Snaith' still scrawled across the wall in spray-paint. Eunice. It takes quite a woman to deliver a decree nisi by singing telegram.

He shuffled through to the kitchen and silverfish scurried from the breadboard as he prodded a loaf blotched with mould as blue as a tradesman's apron. He surveyed the past fortnight's *Oomph!*'s covering his front room floor like the base of a litter tray - and then saw the lumps in the corner. Hell, you try getting to the toilet after 7 Manhattans. Frankly he was amazed he'd even got his trousers down in time.

Snaith scrumpled up a sports page and jammed it in his mouth. Football scores in suitably lacklustre Beef and Onion. The cheerless rozzer mused on what had become of the printed word. A few years back the papers of tomorrow were to be cutting edge, high tech. Continuously refreshed news racing across micrometre thick flexi-screens in electronic ink. And now before him lay the reality. The *Oomph!* had been the first to go edible. Try as they might the others just couldn't ignore the improvement in circulation. Six months on and even the Telegraph made a passable snack, albeit a little gamey for Snaith's palate.

Pictures of the missing infant stared up at him, seemingly as upset as he by the headlines. Every day since the disappearance the front page had been plastered with spuff seemingly made real by repetition.

*'Paedo Foxtrot Bravo - Cops Hunt Totnap Monster'*

*'God takes case - Wembley Mass-Pray blessed by hopeful Pope'*

*'Is Beast Priest: Inside, Satanic Secret of Sicko's Devious Previous'*

Snaith reached about among the newsprint for the last of the strawberry Horoscopes. The Pull-out supplements, they were no better.

*'Is your tot too hot? Are they tempting sickos? Free inside - 'An ugly child is a safe child' poster'.*

*'Is it YOU?! Open YOUR home to the law and eliminate yourself from enquiries...'.*

*'Big Cash Comp - Send in YOUR sketch of sinister Kiddynapper'.*

Snaith no longer knew if the World was getting worse, or if these pricks were just working harder.

THE VATICAN PAPAL LAVATORY.
THE VERY NEXT MORNING.
The 2 Cardinals struggled with the Holy Father, like PG Tips Chimps moving a washing machine. Cardinal Paulo shook the drips from the Pope's tinkle with silver tongs, a guard against any unnatural urge that may arise should the 106-year-old handle his own extremity. After 20 flicks it was deemed safe to move him off the newspapers, the sheets of discarded *Oomph!*s on the floor below reminding them once again of their most pressing problem. For the moment poverty, injustice and hunger must take a back seat.

Two days post-abduction, and at the *Oomph!*'s insistence, the Gaffer had accompanied the missing Tot's forlorn parents to Rome on a mercy-mission-come-photo-shoot. Once again Cardinal Paulo's faux-pas jigged in front of his mind's eye...

THAT MEETING...

Grieving Mother - 'We, we just want you to do what you can'.

Cardinal Paulo - 'I'll make some calls. If a priest has the child we'll take a very dim view indeed...'

An uncomfortable silence before Cardinal Paulo hammered home the Church's intolerance of such behaviour.

'*Very* dim. I can assure you if that is the case it'll be quite some time before they abduct another one...'

Still blank faces. The Cardinal sensed he may have grabbed the wrong end of the stick but ploughed on nonetheless.

'...and if they do, it'll be in some God forsaken outpost in the Third World...'

Then came the jab in the ribs from Cardinal Alphonse. Luckily the Gaffer helpfully chipped in.

'I, I think they mean prayers. Stuff like that'.

'Oh. Yes. Of course. Prayers, right. I was just going to suggest that' mumbled Cardinal Paulo.


BACK IN THE PAPAL LAVATORY

It hadn't been the best P.R. and ever since the Cardinals had followed the story, at first praying, then crossing their fingers for some turn of events for which they could at least take partial credit.

'La Talpa...' croaked the bewildered Pontiff.

The two Cardinals buttoned him up...

'LA TALPA!

...Alphonse popping a couple of sedatives from a blister pack, thankful the public's poor grasp of Latin left them unaware his boss now often preached to a packed St Peter's not only that Jesus would soon return, but that he would do so in the form of a giant mole.

*'Non specta ad caelum... specta ad terram sub pede! (The Latin for 'Look not to the sky... but to the ground beneath your feet')*

They could all do without hearing *that* again.

'We have to face up to the facts', mumbled Cardinal Paulo. 'We... The Church could really use a result here'.

He paused a moment, clearly troubled.

'Alphonse... do you ever think, well... we do all this praying, sometimes quite specific, and...'

'We all have doubts'. Cardinal Alphonse put a tender hand to his colleague. 'But surely it's those doubts that form the bedrock of our faith. *Anyone* can believe in things backed by evidence... things that can be proved. We have *so* much more, because we put our trust in things that have *no* proof. Belief in things without substantiation, surely that is what it takes to be truly divine'.

'You mean things like... La Talpa?'

'Let's call that the exception that proves the rule, eh?' whispered Alphonse.

Both men eyed a recent copy on the floor beneath which showed the parents taking prayers with both a Rabbi and an Imam. Alphonse broke the silence.

'This tiny child... There is a truly terrible outcome that we might yet have to face…'.

Paulo nodded.

'…one of the other lot could find her first. The Muzzies... or that bunch with the elephant with the extra arms'.

At that Alfonse rummaged furiously in his cassock and pulled out his phone.

'That wheezing policeman who brought the parents here. Where's his damn number?!'

THE SQUAD HQ. 9:05am
Outside the Gaffer puffed contentedly on the fire escape while at the table DIs Wilton and Harris tucked into coffee and buns. For the first morning in a month the men felt unfettered by media interference. The door swung open and in strode Snaith. Wilton leapt to his feet shaking crumbs from his coat.

'She's not with you is she, Mel Vernon!?'

'I've a feeling we've got a few hours off', smirked Snaith. He tossed his phone down onto the table to reveal the *Oomph!* website.

'No! Look at that,' gawped Harris, 'Bob Vernon's taken a right beating... undercover beyond the postcode... jumped by a Paedo gang...'

'Brave guy', mumbled Wilton, 'I guess I must have misjudged him'.

'Maybe don't believe all you read', hissed Snaith,

begrudgingly impressed at the Journo's ability to even turn his well-deserved beating to his advantage. He plonked a plastic sack on the tabletop.

'So. This case. What do we know?'

Harris was first.

'Erm... snatched kid, 6 months old... no leads.'

'I said what do we KNOW?!'

The others swapped anxious glances; it had clearly been a long night for Snaith, his eyes bloodshot as one of the Gaffer's sputum samples.

'I popped by their house this morning. Forced the lock. They were out doing another photocall'.

Snaith fumbled with his phone and the tear-stained couple appeared beneath a headline:

*'Down in the dumps? Ten top treats to banish the blues'*

'Well?'

'We know who we're looking for' said Harris pulling a sheaf of photos from the case folder.

'Come on. It's a baby. As was kindly pointed out to me, they all look the 'uckin' same don't they?'

'A *noisy* baby', blurted Wilton. 'There's the recording remember.'

He had a point. Neighbours either side had made repeated complaints to the council about the racket, and had even provided evidence. The little critter certainly had a fine set of lungs.

'Oh yes. That. I've been listening to that'.

Snaith jabbed his phone –

*Waaaah wah waaah wah wah wah waaaaaah waah waaaaaaaaaah wah wah wahhhhhhhhhhhhhhh wah wah awh awhh wahh. Waaaah wah waaah wah wah wah…*

The sound file played for its full length. The Gaffer was the first to twig.

'It's… it's a loop'.

'Quite. And as far as I know babies don't cry in 2 minute loops'.

'But you only have to look at them to know they're kosher' interjected Wilton. 'You saw how she blubbed for the press'.

Snaith pulled a red canvas lace up from the bag and prodded the insole.

'See the blood spots? Drawing pins. Drawing pins in her shoes. It's an old Boy Band trick to turn on the waterworks. Just press down when you do the solo to camera'.

It was a full minute before DI Wilton broke the silence, catching his foot in his pocket trying to scratch his ear in the manner of a cat.

'So... what are you saying?'

'You know what I'm saying. There. Is. No. Baby'.

With that Snaith stuffed a hand into the bag and slapped a wet sponge dome the size of an Olive Ridley Turtle down onto the table.

'Mummy Tummy. Found it in the loft, hidden in the water tank. Think about it, she was up the duff when they moved in- '

'But the birth, medical records...' Wilton clearly couldn't take it all in.

'Home birth... a bent doctor.... It's not rocket science. Think about it, the few times they were seen with their baby... well, they just 'borrowed' one, and I think I know where from. We've been set up'.

All three turned to Snaith.

'But who?'

Who benefits most? The *Oomph!* Think of how much copy those dillocks have got from all this'.

*'Smoke. I must have smoke!'*, roared the Gaffer pulling a blob of Nicorette gum from the grapefruit-sized ball in his cheek and squidging it over the detector. '3 months searching for a child that doesn't exist', he muttered, tearing each end off a pack of 20 and wedging it in his mouth. 'They'll hang us out to dry for this'.

'Handy', said Snaith. 'As we'll be wet through from them pissing on us first'.

## Briiing Briiiiiing!

The Gaffer stared at his phone.

'Bugger. It's that bleeding dago bead jiggler Alphonse again'.

Snaith held out a hand.

'May I? I think I've seen a way out of this'.

116

THE PRESS ROOM. NEW SCOTLAND YARD.
THE NEXT MORNING. 10am.

Snaith would never forget the faces of 'mother' and 'father', when they were 'reunited' with 'their' baby, trading desperate glances as they fumbled with the infant. Surely well remunerated for acting as new parents, but unlike their earlier abduction appeal this time their tears seemed very real. In fact there wasn't a dry eye in the room, mainly thanks to Cardinals Alphonse and Paulo, whisked over from Rome to share a little credit and swinging far too much incense.

THE PRESS ROOM. TWO HOURS LATER.

Bob and Melanie Vernon, drained from a sleepless night, scanned the near-empty room from behind the mics. The public's appetite for child snatch stories had been momentarily sated; it would be at least a month before the press could once more play cat's cradle with the nation's heartstrings.

Not even the *Oomph!* had sent a man, presumably they thought their top reporter partnership capable of covering the abduction of their own baby. And The Squad were certainly nowhere to be seen.

★

A call to the *Oomph!s* proprietor had confirmed Snaith's theory. He was a pragmatic man: the story had had a good innings, and there was still many a column inch to be had from the joyous handover.

It hadn't been the Squad's finest hour, but it wasn't like they'd actually snatched the tot, just bunged the aupere a roll of notes and she'd disappeared back into beyond-postcode London reassured it was all something to do with national security. Then it was just a case of ensuring the infant was discovered swaddled by a font in a sufficiently Catholic church and everything else just fell into place.

It's hardly like they'd had any options. Had the error become known it could have threatened the whole future of the Force. Instead the Squad was free to fight real crime, helped by a colossal back-hander from a grateful Vatican. Besides, how could they tell the public it was all tosh? Even popping out for milk that morning Snaith could see the good news had put a spring in the nation's step. It was the best story for a decade. Who was he to break their hearts?

'Sometimes', thought Snaith, 'To do a good thing you have to do a *very* bad thing'.

## SCOTLAND YARD UNDERGROUND CAR PARK. THAT EVENING.

*'He's coming over'* barked Snaith's earpiece.

Snaith heard shuffling footsteps as the bedraggled reporter approached. They'd all known this was possible. Inevitable.

'You've got to help me', gabbled Bob Vernon. This is going to sound nuts... that kid, the one they, you lot gave back... it's *mine*. Someone took *our* kid'.

'I don't follow'. Snaith tinkered under the bonnet, unable to meet the man's eyes.

'...there was no snatched kid. Never was. It was all a scam... those parents, they were just paid to pretend'. At that Vernon started gabbling. 'You've got to help us, get some DNA or something, it's mine. I know it. Come on, we're old mates aren't we?'

'OK' mumbled the Detective, 'Just as soon as I've sorted this. Know anything about motors?'

Vernon wiped his nose on his sleeve and leaned over.

'There's no fan belt. There should be a fan belt down there... there-ish'.

As the reporter poked under the bonnet Snaith pulled the length of yellow silk from his pocket.

People need to believe in the forces of Law, many crave a strong church. Just this once morale must take precedence over morality thought Snaith as he made busy with the sash from the Baltic State Beauty.

Miss Latvia. Hobbies: walking, movies, collecting pebbles... accomplice to Murder!

CASE CLOSED

# ALL GOOD THINGS...

██████████ CREMATORIUM COMPLEX
THE GENTS. EARLY EVENING.

Detective Inspector Snaith slapped the groaning white box on the wall by the sink - this had to be the only place in London that had escaped the hand dryer revolution of the early Noughties. Stronger blasts blew out candles on retirement home birthday cakes. By the time his hands were dried he was going to need another piss. So he dropped his trousers and wiped them on his underpants. More damp there hardly mattered as they'd already taken quite a hit from his increasingly treacherous urethra.

Outside the Gents he looked warily back down the corridor to the function room. Where 3 dozen coppers toasted the life of a recently departed Chief Inspector –

*'Cummmonn! kneeees-up-muvva-braaaan…'*

- and a familiar voice was hell-bent on kick-starting a sing-a-long. Snaith hated sing-a-longs. Ever since that Karaoke bar where ex-wife Eunice had improvised a 90 minute epic poem about his physical inadequacies to a looping backdrop of 'You Give Love a Bad Name'. The well-irrigated crowd roaring for an encore as he whimpered, cornered by a follow-spot he'd later learned she'd brought by the for rehearsals the day before. The make-up sex had been incredible though. The mattress had squeaked like a pet shop, easily loud enough for him to hear from the spare room.

*'kneezzuppppmuvvva-braaan, unnda tha taybulll*
*yew musss go...'*

It was Sean Murray. AKA Trumpet, surely the gobbiest DI in Greater London. A man capable of transforming any social occasion into just empty hours of performance laughter and monologue swapping.

*'Eeeee-eye-eeee-eyee-eeeeee-eyee-ooooh'*

It had reached critical mass, the others joining in. Snaith turned about and walked to the dark end of the corridor, pushing doors till one opened. Inside it was dusty and quiet, though luckily not in a way that brought further painful reminders of his marital bed. Snaith leant on a shoulder-high stack of metal chairs and studied the floating specks in a shaft of twilight that fell through double doors to a garden beyond.

He shut his eyes and it was 19█ in the Aylesbury Odeon, where his schoolboy self sat captivated by the flickering beam from the projection room. 300 people gasped as Bambi's mother took a bullet. Then his own had dragged him out cackling 'Come on boy, that's the only bit worth seeing'.

Damn flashbacks. So much for a moment's peace. He rummaged in a carrier bag of plunder from the function room, stopping dead on hearing laboured breathing.

'Bit much in there isn't it?'

It was the Gaffer. The Squad's main man, his boss

for the bulk of the past decade.

'I know what you're thinking' he continued from the shadows. 'Yesterday. It wasn't, well… it wasn't 100 per cent by the book'.

'I wouldn't know'. Snaith shuddered at the memory. 'Long time since I've been to a Wake'.

That was true. And being just 8 he'd assumed it was called a Wake in an instructive sense. Only to discover when you tried to do what was suggested all Hell broke loose. Shaking his Auntie Sylvie with the very best of intentions, mistaking her jiggling wig for signs of reanimation. Realising his error he'd tried to slip out through the forest of legs of horrified grown-ups, but the glass eye he'd shaken loose soon saw him hit the deck. Karma.

'He wouldn't have minded you know. Always got on with those lab guys' slurred the Gaffer. 'Though I'll be the first to admit they did get a bit carried away'.

Snaith pictured the coffin. The Chief Inspector's Missus had asked for an open one, but post Post-mortem hangovers had seen him reassembled with such haste and lack of precision that he now had the air of a hastily stuffed rucksack. Bitter-sweet, as in life the Chief had never missed a chance to move along the Homeless. It had put Snaith in mind of a holiday's end, when you could never get everything back into your suitcase.

Before the mourners had arrived they'd tried him face down, only to reveal more evidence of the

Coroner's fondness for a free drink, the Late Chief Inspector's back resembling a Victorian corset hastily donned in a power cut. Fortunately his wife had also specified a stable-door coffin lid, so they'd left the bottom half open to show just from the thighs down, and spun her some guff about it being a tribute to decades of yelling at recruits to polish their shoes.

Snaith hadn't really cared. After all, he'd barely known the guy.

Footsteps outside, along with the sound of hooves on parquet flooring and in shuffled the eternally-sickly DI Harris followed by the scampering cosmetically adjusted absurdity of DI Wilton.

'Sorry for the tardiness', wheezed Harris, leaning on a wall for support. 'Flowers. Pollen. Allergy'.

'He wasn't juss an ol' bastard you know'. The Gaffer was off again 'He liked a laugh. Remember Stop-and-Search Top Trumps?'

Snaith smiled. He'd played it only last week. You each pick a member of the public and have them empty their wallet. Whoever's choice has the least cash has to get the chips in. Random nonsense but it meant in order to win many cops had switched their attentions to harassing the evidently wealthy, which had at least drawn some heat off of the Black community.

'...that was one of his. Long career too. Started out the week they brought in Ruth Ellis. Last woman to be hung she was...' The Gaffer checked himself, sobering a little and speaking now as though parroting and edict. 'Or so they thought back in those unenlightened times. As we all know from that last training day it's perfectly possible for a woman to be hung. And well hung at that'.

'Don't go there boss' said Snaith. 'It's way too easy for poorly thought-through remarks to be taken the wrong way right now. But for the best possible reasons of course'.

The Gaffer jabbed a finger at no one in particular.

'And he was proper early with all this diversity lark too. Women, Ethnics, our Irish friends... he'd happily fit any one of 'em up. And before a white guy, so don't come it with this institutional racism guff'.

Snaith steadied the wrinkled fool and sat him on what seemed to be a piano stool, albeit one without a piano. The old man frowned, as though a troubling thought had surfaced like bubbles in a shared romantic bath.

'Gennelmen. Gennelmen. Take a seat gennelmen'.

DI Wilton began panting as his big sorrowful eyes darted from The Gaffer to a chair. Back to the Gaffer, back to the chair...

'Yes, OK. But juss for today'.

Snaith sighed as, tail wagging, Wilton clambered onto it.

'Boss. It's just going to make it harder to keep him off the couch at the Station'.

The Gaffer waved away the comment and took a

deep breath.

'There's... there's something I never told you. About us. Well you. The Squad ~'.

The three detectives turned as one to face him.

'~ We are anything but a standard police unit'.

Not this 'we're not normal' crap again thought Snaith, as he scratched a grateful DI Wilton behind his leathery rear-ward facing ear flaps. The Gaffer up-ended some gin, suckling at the bottle like a baby lamb.

'Well, the Chief's gone now...' he whispered -

At the sound of a smashed glass and a cheer from down the hall the Gaffer took unsteadily to his feet and pulled the door tight shut. The Squad found themselves alone. Apart from each other.

'...and when tha' happnn'd my instructions were, well... they were to tell you the truth'.

'The truth?' uttered Snaith. He lowered his bulk onto a chair, and a tear finally came. As he realised he'd pressed flat the mushroom Volly Vents stowed in his back pockets. The Gaffer once more inverted the Gin.

'The truth?!', gasped Harris, fumbling with his inhaler.

Snaith deflowered a vase, as in removed dying flowers from one, not had sex with it. That had been... well, it was what you might call a 'one off'. Albeit it had happened 4 or 5 times. He had been so lonely since Eunice had left. And, he couldn't deny, while they were together. He put the vase to the Gaffer's lips, and the old man knocked back the pint or so of cloudy water and rallied.

'Know what?' He slurred, 'I don't have to tell you. You try and work it out... Detectives... and I'm pretty sure you'll soon get to the bottom of this. Clue clue clue... let's just say the RUC weren't the only Cloppers who spent the early 70s firing off a few too many live rounds'. (*RUC - Royal Ulster Constabulary. The police force of Northern Ireland following Ireland's 1922 partition, until 2001*).

Puzzled looks were exchanged. Though Snaith's was artifice - he'd already twigged, but wanted to watch things play out.

## 20 MINUTES LATER

The random suggestions had come thick and fast from DIs Harris and Wilton, but the next was clearly a favourite as Harris spoke with undisguised smugness.

'We are... Genetically modified crime-fighting mutants!'

'No. No. No', mumbled the Gaffer. 'Did you never wonder about our stunningly low detection rate?.. ...think about it. It's only really Snaith here that ever brings anyone decent in'.

'Of course' declared DI Wilton, leaping from the chair and squatting neatly on his rump, paws on the floor between his splayed hind legs.

'We are an elite force ...'

'Elite?! HAHAHAHAHAHA!' roared the Gaffer. 'Hahahahahahahahaha'

'OK then... Got it!' continued Wilton. 'We are Genetically Modified cri... ah. You just said that didn't you Harris?'

'I did. Yes'.

Snaith chuckled knowingly, and lay on his back on the floor, thumbs hooked behind braces as though the very World itself was his rucksack.

'Last clue', the Gaffer was weary now, all fun gone from his voice. 'Let's just say it was fitting that that service contained so much action from the organ.

'The Organ?'

'Huh?'

'Do I have to paint you a picture?'

DIs Harris and Wilton swapped baffled looks.

'Well, as a matter of fact I already have. Crayons anyhow'. The Gaffer lit his next cigarette from the nub of the current and tossed a scrap of paper.

'Well, I got that Police Artist to. He's got the Chief down to a tee, but he had to guess at your mum Harris as he'd not met her. Her beret... that was my idea'.

As Harris and Wilton stared at the crayon sketch of DI Harris's late mother being seen-to up against a water-cooler the Gaffer sniggered.

'That neither you two, Harris or Wilton even came close to a decent guess... perhaps should have been a hint a little nepotism may have shoved you upwards through the ranks. Detectives! Ha! The very idea!!'

Snaith pulled out the order of service and looked at the face on the front. Remembering a distant figure. On the brief occasions they'd met the Chief had always dodged eye contact. Then there was that time he'd turned up when Snaith was on a stake-out to give him crisps and lemonade. Or when he'd braced himself for demotion after 15 Porch-crawlers had seen him try and beat a confession out of a raincoat dangling from a hat stand, but had only received a smack on the back of the legs. It would also certainly explain why when the Chief had presented him his Police Service Medal it had come with a folded note and a whispered 'here's a fiver, don't tell your mother'.

The crematorium oven meant it was too late to confirm forensically. But Snaith didn't need to. He was suddenly sure if he wanted a DNA sample that matched his real Dad's, he just had to blow his nose. Did it mean his whole career had been a lie? He felt the Gaffer's arm round his shoulder.

'You OK lad?'

Snaith's cogs turned. 'Of course Boss. And Eunice! The only reason that woman treated me like dirt was that he employed her as a training tool. To harden me up for some greater purpose'.

'No son. My guess is she just hates you. But one thing you should remember. Him and your mother… it was actually quite a beautiful thing'.

It may have been just kindness but Snaith was

nonetheless warmed by the words.

'At least it was when they did it in the office. You know we were the first station in the UK to install glass partitions'. The Gaffer pulled out another piece of paper. 'That artists guy's pretty good look –'

Snaith, not sure he could face a crayon likeness of his mother in union with the late Chief Inspector, pushed it away. Though it certainly seemed no less plausible than the other earlier-recounted paternity claim that a cynic might now mistake for literary convenience. (*See 'In Plod We Trust' earlier in this book*)..

'Lads. He gave me things for you, you know. Something to remember him by'.

The Gaffer handed the stunned DI Harris a silver pocket watch, and, after thinking hard about quite where to put it, slid a spotless MET cap badge into DI Wilton's tummy pouch. Then he turned to Snaith.

'He always knew you had what it takes though lad. Not for you baubles and trinkets, he wanted me to pass on the most important lesson he could think of'. With that the Gaffer slapped Snaith hard across the face.

*'Afffafuggssake!'*

'Never... drop your guard Son'.

The Gaffer addressed them all now, as though the entire litre of Gin had left his system, not just the cupful clearly dotting the front of his slacks.

'So. It just remains for me to clean up what I can of his mess, and I need you three to help me...' The

Gaffer stopped short, opened the door, glanced out, then pulled it firmly shut. '…to help me fudge some of his…' the Gaffer gestured to the three men, '…indiscretions.'

'Sure'

'Of course'

'hmmmphnfff!' mumbled Snaith through his hand in pained agreement.

'…by which I mean… take early retirement'.

'Early? How early?' Ventured Snaith, mopping the claret from his left nostril.

'In 20… 25 minutes. That should do it. Thing is there'll be a new Chief along next week. Bound to ask questions. Full pensions for you. Don't kick up a fuss, no one's going to believe you. Besides, any incriminating files. As of an hour ago… well, let's just say we wont be seeing them again'.

It dawned on Snaith why the corpse had seemed so overstuffed.

'That reminds me, I'd better fish what's left of that stapler out of the urn' added the Gaffer looking to the sky 'sorry Charlie, genuine accident, no disrespect intended'.

The big man approximated some kind of genuflection that deployed a hard blowing of his nose as the top of the cross, then continued.

'So get back to the station with a bin bag and - I really don't mean this as some kind of hurtful innuendo – unlike your old man make sure you leave nothing behind that could cause problems in the future, eh?' With that the Gaffer necked the final nug of Gin and, as though a tremendous weight had finally lifted, rested himself by the chest on the piano stool, to look in the dimness to all the World like a suited tortoise.

'If it's any comfort', he whispered, 'he was at East Midlands and Manchester before, so if you're ever in Derby, Leicester, Stockport… wherever, there could well be a sibling or two you could doss down with'.

★

A full minute's silence was broken by Snaith grabbing his carrier bag. He patted Wilton's paw and shook Harris's hand before heading for the double doors.

A few more things made sense now, not least his half-brothers behind him. Maybe their unfortunate origins were the reason he'd always thought their characters in one case rather absurd, and in the other, quite thinly drawn.

THE MEMORIAL GARDENS OUTSIDE.
MOMENTS LATER

Snaith clanked through the wet grass stopping at a bird bath, his eyes chasing the scattering tits – must have been 'bring your son to work' day when they were named – before up-ending his bag. He shook the whisky bottle into the concrete bowl as though it were cold ketchup, juiced 4 lemons with his bare hands and threw in the handful of sugar cubes he'd stuffed in his pocket. Then, like an itchy bear, he leant his broad back against the flimsy tree that housed the birds and shook. A moment later the nest tumbled down beside him, and he took the two remaining eggs from the mess and was soon draining their whites into the bird bath. A crab apple would have to do for decor, but considering the circumstances it looked to him like a pretty good Whisky Sour. With the nosebleed from the Gaffer's lesson adding a generous touch of strawberry blush he drank briskly to the bottom.

Tottering off he left the small garden, slapped the arse of his panda car, then found himself by the bin store facing a pile of black bags that called to him like scatter cushions. At that his legs gave way.

## CASE CLOSED

### POST SCRIPT

DI Snaith was later reinstated. Hence the next collection of his adventures:

#### 'More Tales from the Casebook'

However it was bittersweet. As his appeal only succeeded because, after prising a barnacle of gum from the underside of the Chief's desk, he was able to prove his own DNA wasn't in fact a match at all.

# EPILOGUE

Forty-eight hours of disjointed ramblings and now ex DI Snaith, face flat in a bowl of maraschino cherries, lay wheezing like a rusty kazoo. It was clear I was no longer in the company of a crime-fighter at the top of his game.

Autumn twilight, orange as Jaffa Cake jelly, sputtered through leaves that seemed determined to slap some sense into the run-down cabin. The Dictapod's light flickered, fuel cell now emptier than a bad busker's cap. Yet the job seemed barely half done. We'd not yet broached his 'retirement', this Napoleonic exile... in fact he'd spent the last hour pitching a quiz show based on the Periodic Table, staggering from a back room wrapped in a black plastic cape: 'Boron' writ large across the back in white gloss paint (Its atomic number 5 scrawled beneath).

But it felt like time to go. Cocktail parasols crunched underfoot as I edged to the door, past this most disobedient of public servants, and stumbled into the chill forest beyond. At the sound of twigs snapping underfoot, down by the shore Elmer, the lop-sided teen who's father had rented me the boat, nodded. He tossed down his puzzle-book and yanked the strap on the outboard.

*Thruppppah! Thruppppah! Thruppppah!*

The blades chewed the water and we took leave of the stagnant cove, along with our unwelcome gnat Afros. Tumbling to the slats by my feet the recorder sprang back to life, bouncing into the recent past, Snaith momentarily joining us in the boat.

*'...Men are but wool. They catch on events and unravel. If they're lucky love, tenderness, friendship... these things will knit them into new and stronger shapes...'*

Back in town by midnight. God willing. But would I have chance to return?

## THE END

Contact the author at mrdanevans@hotmail.com
For all the latest DI Snaith news go to danevans.info